Cover Art by Sleepy Fox Studio

❀ Created with Vellum

TRICKY TREATING

TWILIGHT HOLLOW - BOOK THREE

SARA CHRISTENE

CHAPTER ONE

Logan leaned back in his seat, processing what I had just told him. He sipped his coffee, watching me. The lunch rush had ended, so we had the cafe to ourselves.

I fiddled with my coffee cup. "Is there something you don't understand?"

He lifted dark brows and pursed his lips, highlighting his strong cheekbones. "I'm just surprised. You would think as a witch that Halloween would be your favorite holiday."

I leaned my elbows on the table and stared into his dark eyes, willing him to not jump to such silly conclusions. "Logan, on Halloween the veil to the spirit world thins. I'm a channeling witch. Think about it."

His jaw fell open for a moment, then clicked shut.

"I hadn't thought about that," he admitted. "So the myths surrounding Halloween are true?"

I shrugged, then pushed the sleeves of my chunky orange sweater up to my elbows. "I can't speak for all the myths, but the veil does thin. Samhain is the midpoint between the fall equinox and winter solstice. Three nights where spirits can travel freely. If I could run and hide, I would." I watched his hand reaching for the pocket inside his suit jacket. "If you pull out that little notebook, I'm going to smack you."

He grinned, placing his hand back around his coffee cup. "You can't blame me for wanting to remember things. Not when your *world* keeps popping up in my murder investigations. Will Halloween really be that bad for you?"

I shrugged again. "Who can say? This is my first one since I discovered my . . . gifts."

"Are you in danger?"

I thought about it. "I don't think so. Normal ghosts can't hurt you unless you let them. They may be more active around me, but I should be fine." I looked at his suit and his neatly combed black hair. "So are you on your way to an investigation now? You usually don't stop by at this time of day."

He swilled the last of his coffee, then stood. "Nice try, I'm not involving you in any more murders."

I lifted a brow as I looked up at him. "So you're saying there was a murder?"

"Thanks for the coffee, Adelaide. I'll see you around." He hesitated. "You're sure you're going to be fine?"

I nodded. "I'd be more than fine if you didn't leave me dying from curiosity."

He smirked. "Better than actually dying." He gave me a wave and went for the door before I could argue further.

I watched him go, then glanced around the cafe for Spooky, finding him watching me from the top one of the bookshelves lined with used books. I would have asked him what he thought about the looming threat of Halloween, but he'd gone back to not speaking to me. Or maybe I'd gone back to not listening. I had spent my whole life only listening with my ears, it was no small feat to learn to listen with my mind. I wasn't sure I would ever get the hang of it.

With a sigh, I stood, taking my empty coffee cup back behind the counter. I had an hour before Richie came in, and I needed to refill the barren display cases with cookies and bagels. Not many people wanted pastries and muffins after lunch, but cookies and bagels were always in demand. The bagels had been a new addition, and they sure weren't easy to make. Richie had been insisting we add sandwiches to the menu too, but I was spread so thin as it was, there was just no way.

I needed help with all of the baking, but my baked goods only sold well because they were imbued with positive magic. If anyone else took over the baking, they wouldn't be as good. My only other option was to spend even less time at the cafe, but part of why I loved my work so much was interacting with my regulars. I wasn't quite ready to give it up.

My mood quickly souring, I braided my ginger curls to fall down my back, slipped on some disposable gloves, and started restocking the cases. I supposed I could just keep having a limited number of baked goods every day. It would work during the off-season, but during times when camping, hunting, or skiing were in full swing, I just couldn't keep up. I loved my regulars, but tourism was what kept me in business.

The bell on the door rang. My eyes darted upward, then narrowed. The cafe was empty, just me and Spooky.

Figuring I had imagined it, I went back to work. I had just placed the final snickerdoodle in the case when a shiver went up my spine. I froze mid-motion, then slowly looked to my left. Nothing, but I could have sworn I sensed something. I turned around, placing the empty tray near the industrial espresso machine.

"Hi, Addy," a girl's voice said to my back.

I whirled around, grabbing a pair of metal tongs to protect myself.

A teenaged ghost watched me with her hands on her hips. She wore colorless flared jeans, and a boxy t-shirt with her hair in braided pigtails. "What are you gonna do with those?" she asked, nodding toward the tongs. "Pinch me to death?"

I just stared at her, frozen with the tongs in my hand.

She shrugged. "I suppose it might work, if I weren't already dead."

"Ida?" I gasped, recognizing her from my mom's old photo albums. Suddenly I could picture her colorless braids as strawberry blonde, and her eyes chocolate brown like Luna's. She looked about thirteen, but I knew she was actually sixteen. The age that she was when she died. While she and I had technically *met* before, I didn't think she could take such a solid form.

"You seem surprised to see me."

I finally managed to lower the tongs, dropping them lightly onto the counter. "Of course I'm surprised to see you. How are you here? *Why* can I see you?"

She floated toward the counter. "Have you looked at a calendar lately? It's almost Halloween."

I leaned forward on my elbows, pinched my brow,

and shook my head. "Please don't tell me I'm going to be seeing all the ghosts around as clearly as you."

"That's why I'm here. I know it's your first Halloween since you came into your powers. I hate to break it to you, but it's going to be a doozy."

"A doozy?" I asked weakly, lifting my head.

She nodded. "I was twelve when I came into my powers. My first Halloween scared me out of my wits."

I stifled a groan. She'd been a child when she discovered her powers. Why had it taken me so long?

Spooky hopped up on the counter, startling me. He slunk toward Ida's ghost, purring loudly.

She petted him. "Hey there, little buddy, long time no see." Where her hand smoothed over his back, the black fur shifted.

My eyes flew wide. "Ida, how are you actually touching him?"

She gave me a mischievous grin. "Like I said, Halloween is going to be a real doozy."

The bell on the door rang again, and this time it wasn't a ghost. Richie walked inside, none-the-wiser to the conversation I'd been having.

When I glanced back to Ida, she was gone.

Spooky hopped off the counter and trotted toward Richie as he shucked his leather coat. "Sorry I'm so early," he was saying. "My professor was sick today."

Finally he looked up to me as he reached the register. "Geez, Addy, you look like you've seen a ghost."

I shook my head and pushed away from the counter. "You have no idea. Since you're early, do you want to take over from here?"

I was already grabbing my coat and bag before he could answer.

"Sure, Addy, but are you sure you're okay?"

I forced a smile as I put on my tan wool coat. "Totally fine, I just remembered I was supposed to do something for Luna. Evie will come by this evening to lock up."

"All right," he said hesitantly, smoothing a hand over his slicked back black hair. "As long as you're sure nothing's wrong."

I picked up Spooky on my way around the counter. "I'll see you later." I kept smiling so much that it made my cheeks hurt, but I didn't want to worry him.

I didn't want to tell him how wrong things suddenly were. Because if I could see and talk to a long dead ghost like Ida, then I was about to see a whole lot more.

I'd known Halloween was going to be stressful, but I hadn't realized it was going to be a real . . . doozy.

CHAPTER TWO

I called Luna on the way home, glad I hadn't walked to work. I drove most days now. There just wasn't any other way to transport my baked goods unless Evie picked them up before her shift. I missed my walks. They were a nice way to unwind between work and home.

I pulled up my driveway and hurried inside with Spooky, wanting a moment to clean up my kitchen before Luna arrived. All of my baking trays and mixing bowls were still in the sink, and the countertops were smudged with flour and butter. Luna would surely bring Callie, and I had a feeling once they both arrived there wouldn't be time for cleaning.

I had just leaned the final pan against the drying rack when a knock sounded on the front door.

I hurried out of the kitchen and through the living

room to answer it, finding both my sisters standing outside. I let out a breath I hadn't realized I'd been holding. "I was worried you'd call mom too."

Callie's strawberry blonde curls were flat and frizzy on one side. She'd probably been taking a nap when Luna roused her after my phone call. "Yeah right. Cousin Amber is still over there."

I stepped aside as Callie walked past, then turned to regard Luna.

Her chocolate brown eyes danced with mischief. "We both agreed we shouldn't call in mom and Amber unless things get serious. None of us need that added . . . stress in our lives." She walked past me, leaving a cloud of lavender in her wake.

I shut the door, then turned toward my sisters as they both shucked their coats and slumped down onto my white sofa. I really hoped it would be like Luna said, that things wouldn't get too serious, but I doubted it. Ida had been able to pet Spooky. I wasn't worried about her, she was a friendly ghost, but there were plenty of less than friendly things around. Things like an evil dark magic intent on possessing me.

I walked toward my sisters as Spooky strutted into the room. He waited for me to sit on one of the adjacent chairs before hopping onto my lap. Both of my sisters watched me expectantly.

I had only told Luna over the phone that Ida had visited me, and that I was worried about Halloween.

I sighed. "Okay, long story short, I think any ghosts around me are going to have a lot more power this Halloween than they should normally have. Ida was able to pet Spooky. If the dark magic is some form of ghost or spirit, it's going to be more powerful around me too. It's already capable of possession. If there were a time for it to strike, it would be over the next few days."

Luna nodded along with my words, draping thick auburn hair over her sweater-clad shoulder. "I think you're right. We all thought it had gone quiet because with cousin Amber around, we have a full coven. But maybe it was just biding its time knowing Halloween was near."

Callie leaned back against the cushions, her red plaid flannel a stark contrast to all the white. Her eyes were on Luna. "But what can we do about it? She's a channeling witch." She gestured to me. "Her power attracts spirits. Her connection to them can give them solid form on this earth. There's no way to sever it or prevent it."

Luna gave me a motherly smile, though she was only a couple years older than me. "We'll just put up wards and stick with Addy until Halloween is over."

"You mean I'll stick with Addy," Callie said tersely.

"It may be the slow season for me, but you still have all of your patients."

Luna rolled her eyes. "I've had my schedule cleared around Halloween for weeks now." She looked back and forth between the two of us. "Honestly, had neither of you been worried until now? I thought of this the moment we found out Addy is a channeling witch."

My phone buzzing on the coffee table saved me from answering. In truth, I hadn't really thought about it until a few days ago, and then hadn't realized just how dire things might become. I'd had so many pleasant Halloweens in my life, I just couldn't envision it being otherwise.

I leaned forward and grabbed my phone, seeing Logan's name on the caller ID. Holding my finger up to keep my sisters from talking for a moment, I answered it. "My my, two times in one day, to what do I owe the pleasure, detective?"

"You remember earlier when I said I wasn't involving you in any more murder investigations?" Logan asked.

I nodded, though he couldn't see it. "Yes, go on."

"Well I lied. I think this murder requires your . . . expertise."

While part of me enjoyed making Logan a liar, my

mouth suddenly went dry. "Do you think it was the necromancer?"

We hadn't seen the necromancer again since he evaded the police. We still didn't even know his name, but I had a feeling he'd be back at some point.

"Maybe, or maybe it's just a coincidence," Logan answered. "Either way, it's clear my victim thought she was a witch, and her murder looks ritualistic."

My pulse picked up. Both my sisters were leaning forward as if they might catch Logan's end of the conversation.

"*Thought* she was a witch?" I asked.

"Spell books, crystals, an athame, you name it. She has the whole kit."

My breath eased out of me. It was rare to meet another real witch, she could just be Wiccan, but, "What was her name?"

"I really shouldn't tell you. I could get in enormous trouble for even telling you as much as I have."

I leaned back in my seat, absentmindedly petting Spooky. "If you want my help, you're going to have to tell me."

Silence. I could picture him chewing the inside of his cheek, annoyed because I was right. "I'll come over. I'd rather not do this over the phone."

"Luna and Callie are here."

Another weighted pause. "I'll be there in thirty

minutes, but we'll speak in private, and you have to promise not to tell them anything."

I looked at Luna and Callie's expectant faces and knew I would have a fight on my hands, but I understood. He was already taking a huge risk in divulging information on an active murder investigation to me. "Deal. I'll see you soon."

He hung up without saying goodbye, and I lowered my phone to my lap. I looked first at Callie, then Luna. "You know I can't tell you guys anything."

Luna's eyes narrowed. Suddenly her mothering nature was gone, replaced with the shadow self that made no one want to mess with her. "If a witch was murdered, we need to know."

I was glad she was my sister, because Luna could be . . . scary.

"We don't even know if she was a real witch," I countered. "Let me talk to Logan, and if I think it's something you should know about, I'll convince him to let me tell you."

Callie relaxed against the sofa. "That's fair enough, I suppose. Now can we eat something? I'm starving."

Luna watched me for a moment longer, then nodded her assent. "Alright, I'll let it go for now, and I'll trust you to tell us if it's important." She gave me a small smile. "And I second Callie's request."

I checked the time on my phone. It was almost 4

o'clock. Since everyone was hungry we could have an early dinner at five. If Logan was already coming over, I might as well feed him.

I put my phone on the table and stood. "Let's have some wine while we cook. I have a feeling we're going to need it."

My sisters followed me into the kitchen. They were never much help with the cooking, but it was nice to have the company. I wondered when Ida would show up again, or maybe she was waiting until I was alone. If that was the case, she was out of luck. I knew my sisters, and I wouldn't be alone until after Halloween was over.

It was going to be a rough few days. I could only hope we were all up for it.

CHAPTER THREE

Logan arrived just as I was finishing up dinner. I had made enough chicken piccata to have leftovers, along with roasted vegetables, salad, and rolls. Callie had put together a charcuterie board with leftover cheese and other items from my fridge, along with some of our mom's homemade boysenberry jam.

I uncorked a second bottle of wine as Luna left the kitchen to let Logan in.

A moment later, I heard his voice. "Mmm, something smells good."

Luna's warm laugh echoed through the house. "It's always wise to visit a kitchen witch around breakfast or dinner time."

I frowned at the term as I sprinkled a little sea salt onto the roasted veggies. Not that there was anything

I put a hand on his shoulder, appreciating how much he cared about his work. For Logan, it wasn't about the prestige or pride. He just truly cared about justice. It was something we had in common. "Start from the beginning. My sisters can wait."

HE TOLD ME EVERYTHING, though there wasn't as much to tell as I'd hoped. The victim's name was Alison. I didn't recognize her surname. Part of me was glad I didn't recognize it, because it wouldn't make me feel any guiltier about keeping things from my sisters, but at the same time, it also didn't help the case.

The rest of the details gave me little more to go on. A dead woman, late twenties, found in her home with mysterious symbols scrawled around her in blood. Lots of witch paraphernalia, but no murder weapon, no fingerprints, and the neighbors hadn't heard or seen a thing.

I knew the only way I was going to be able to help was to go to the scene of the crime. If there were any ghosts around, I could question them.

Logan had decided that task was better left until tomorrow, once the rest of the crime scene unit had cleared out. So that just left us to face two nosy witches at dinner.

We were walking downstairs as someone knocked on the door.

I froze. "*Crap.*"

"What is it?" Logan asked behind me.

The surprise of seeing Ida earlier had made me forget one very important detail. "I was supposed to have a date with Max tonight. I forgot to cancel."

"I can leave," Logan said blandly.

I shook my head. "No, that still leaves a massive dinner and my sisters to explain. I have an idea, just go with it."

I went down the last few steps, wishing I had changed out of my orange sweater into something nicer, then moved toward the door. This wasn't the first time I had forgotten about a date with Max. In fact, tonight was a rescheduled date after I'd gotten wrapped up in a visit with a friendly spirit a few nights prior. She had been newly dead, a ghost just preparing to move on and wanting me to explain what was happening to her.

I reached the door and opened it, a smile already plastered on my face.

Max stood outside, a bouquet of roses in his hand. Beneath his winter coat he wore a hunter green button up that made his brown eyes look hazel. Charcoal slacks and loafers completed the look. He had dressed up for a nice date, and here I was in my ugliest sweater and jeans.

My guilt increased tenfold.

"Something smells good," he said as he stepped inside, making no comment on my outfit of choice.

"Surprise!" I lifted my hands, hoping my act was convincing. "I decided to throw us a dinner party tonight so you could get to know my sisters better."

Max turned his attention to Logan, still standing near the base of the stairs.

I'd been so nervous coming up with my lie—I'd always been a terrible liar—that I'd forgotten to come up with a story for Logan's presence. I hesitated, wondering whether or not I should shut the door. If Logan was about to leave, it would seem weird if I shut it.

Logan smoothly stepped forward and shook Max's hand. "I should probably apologize for weaseling my way into this affair. When I stopped by the cafe earlier and Addy said she was having a dinner party, I couldn't resist the opportunity to try her cooking. If it's anything like her baking, we are both in for a treat."

The knot in my stomach eased. In truth, Logan had tried my cooking before, but I appreciated him covering for me. I shut the door and stepped up beside Max.

The lies were already making me ill with nerves,

but I didn't want Max to know that I had forgotten yet another date. It would've been so much easier if he knew that I was a witch, so I could give him a legitimate reason for why I had forgotten. But I couldn't exactly tell him my long dead aunt had visited my cafe earlier.

Callie peeked her head out of the kitchen. "Perfect timing. The table is all set for five."

For once I was glad my sisters were expert eavesdroppers. She had heard everything and caught on. Callie motioned for Logan to come into the kitchen, and he quickly obeyed.

I took the roses from Max and kissed him on the cheek, coming away with the faint scent of aftershave. "I hope this is okay."

He grinned. "No, it's great. I love that you want me to get to know your sisters."

Guilt. Guilt. Guilt. I smiled. "Let's go then, dinner is all ready."

He led the way into the kitchen and I let my smile slip. If we were going to continue dating, I would eventually have to tell him my secret. It was inevitable, but I was still terrified. Logan had taken the news surprisingly well, but I wasn't dating Logan. I had technically been lying to Max the entire time we'd been seeing each other—which admittedly wasn't long, but still, not a great way to start a potential relationship.

As we went through the kitchen and toward my dining table, I had to admit the real reason I was scared. Max was a practical man, he didn't believe in ghosts or magic. I wasn't worried about him believing me—I had ways to prove it to him—but it was a very real possibility he would simply refuse to accept it. If that happened, the short-lived relationship was over.

Of course, I probably didn't need to be worrying about the future when I had enough problems in the present. Fingers crossed we could get through this dinner party without any ghostly visitors or letting any secrets slip.

After I put the roses in a vase on the kitchen counter, Max held out a chair for me, and as I sat I happened to glance out the large window into my darkening backyard. There was the white silhouette of a teenage girl standing there. Noticing me watching her, she approached the glass, grinned, and gave me a wave.

Well . . . crap.

CHAPTER FOUR

Ibarely noticed as we passed steaming platters of food around the table, though I did notice that they were all steaming, as if they had just come out of the oven. It was a small charm Luna had performed at many a family gathering. A dash of fire magic, and food would be piping hot at any time. Of course, the magic did have its limits. Reheated coffee still tasted like reheated coffee.

I dared another glance out the window as the roasted veggies made their way to me, but Ida was gone. Spooky had gone off somewhere else in the house. Was he with her right now? I couldn't think of a good excuse to go looking, except going to the bathroom, and I was saving that excuse in case I needed it later.

I took a small serving of vegetables, then handed

the platter to Max on my right. Luna sat on my left, and Callie was already talking Logan's ear off at the other end of the table.

As we all ate and fell into comfortable conversation I began to relax. Maybe Ida had just been letting me know she was here, and would wait until the mundanes cleared out.

Luna was in the middle of telling Max about the trials of opening your own therapy practice when the butter dish floated up from the middle of the table.

I stopped breathing as Callie leapt from her seat and grabbed it, knocking the table with her thighs and sending other dishes rattling.

Max and Luna both turned to find Callie staring dumbly back at them, clutching the butter dish in two hands.

Callie extended the dish toward Max, a nervous grin taking up half her face. "I can't remember if we offered you any butter."

Max glanced down at his half-eaten dinner. "Um, I'm fine, thank you."

"I'll take some," Logan interrupted, standing to pry the dish from Callie's hands.

Luna looked from Logan to Callie, then laughed. "Our mother was always strict with table manners," she said to Max, regaining his attention and ending the awkward moment.

Callie and Logan both gave me, *what the hell was that?* looks.

I shook my head slightly. I hadn't seen what lifted the butter dish, but I had a feeling Ida had gotten bored with waiting for the mundanes to leave.

Callie and Logan lowered their gazes to the table as Max's fork lifted beside his turned shoulder.

Logan slowly reached for the fork, then retracted his hand as a black blur leapt from the ground and knocked it out of the air.

Max turned as both the cat and the fork hit the floor.

"You're no fun, Spooky," I heard Ida lecture from somewhere behind me.

I wanted to look for her, but Max had turned his attention to me. "Are you all right, Addy? You look like you're about to be sick."

As he asked it, Ida appeared right behind him, making funny faces at his back.

I stood abruptly. "Too much wine," I explained.

Acting on instinct, I reached behind Max and grabbed Ida's arm, and I mean I actually *grabbed* it, then dragged her away from the table and through the kitchen.

She cursed and complained all the way across the living room and up the stairs as I tried to listen to my sisters covering for me back at the table.

Their words faded as I reached my bedroom, then dragged the ghost inside, finally letting her go. A fine trembling had set into my shoulders.

While I had a few choice things to say to Ida, my primary thought came out first. "How in the hell did I actually just manage to grab you? You're a ghost. I shouldn't be able to touch you."

Ida crossed her arms and scowled at me. "Halloween, Addy. Plus I'm the ghost of a witch. I'm stronger than mundane spirits when the veil is thin."

I took a few deep breaths, waiting for the trembling to subside. When it didn't, I raked my fingers through my loose curls. "So other ghosts won't be like you, right? They won't be able to touch things." I glared at her. "Or *move* things from the dinner table with mundanes present."

She narrowed her eyes. "You're no fun, Addy. Don't you know how long it's been since I last got to prank mundanes?"

"I'd say it's only been about a year."

She shook her head. "No, Addy, being around you now that you've found your powers makes me stronger. I haven't been this strong since I died. And to answer your question, other ghosts shouldn't be able to do as much as I can, though they still will be stronger around you. Maybe they could move a few things around if they tried hard enough. If you run into the ghost of another witch though, you might want to watch out."

"Addy?" Callie's voice called up the stairs.

I winced. "I don't have time for this right now," I whispered. "Can you stay up here and behave yourself until Max leaves?"

"Why not just tell him about me?" she asked. "The other mundane knows, he seems fine with it."

"I'm not dating the other mundane," I growled. "Now stay up here, or I'll banish you myself."

I walked past her and out the bedroom door. It was far past time to fake a stomach ache, and I'd simply have to avoid Max until Halloween was over. Anything else would simply be too stressful.

"Kill joy," I heard Ida grumble as I started down the stairs.

In that moment I sympathized with every mom who had to deal with teenagers. Suddenly I was glad that all I had was a cat. He was trouble enough.

CHAPTER FIVE

I walked Max to the door while my sisters and Logan cleaned up the table.

He put his hands on my shoulders and looked down at me. "Are you sure you'll be alright? I can stay and help clean up."

I shook my head. "It's probably just a migraine, I'll be fine. Let the others handle the mess. I know you get up early."

The little frown mark between his eyebrows deepened. "You get up early too, Addy. Are you sure you aren't pushing yourself too hard? I don't even know how you had the energy to cook this whole dinner tonight. With everything you do at the cafe, you must be exhausted."

"More than you know," I sighed.

He moved one hand from my shoulder to tuck a

curl behind my ear. "Maybe you should take a few days off. Rest up. I could make you dinner."

Normally I would have argued, but given recent events, it was probably not a good idea for me to be in the Toasty Bean surrounded by mundanes. "Maybe you're right. I'll still have to do all the baking, but I'm sure I could get Evie and Richie to cover everything else."

His expression was a mixture of bemusement and wonder.

I put my hands on my hips. "Why are you looking at me like that?"

He grinned. "You agreed with me so easily."

"I'm not that difficult," I muttered.

He kissed me on the cheek. "Yes, you are. I'll let you get to bed." He put his hand on the door knob. "Call me in the morning?"

I nodded. The night had been all too bizarre, and he wasn't even questioning me. I smiled at him as he opened the door, though I kept it muted since I was playing sick. "Talk to you in the morning."

He gave me a wave, then was out the door.

I shut it softly behind him.

"It's about time," Ida said to my back. "I thought you would be saying your goodbyes *forever*."

I turned around. "I left you in the bedroom ten minutes ago, stop complaining."

Logan and Callie came into the room from the kitchen, the former following my gaze and narrowing his eyes in Ida's direction.

I looked to Callie. "I'm assuming you filled him in?"

She shrugged. "The truth seemed easier than anything else I could think of to explain what happened."

Logan was still looking in Ida's general direction. "There's a ghost in here, right?" He looked to me.

I walked across the room to stand next to Ida. "Logan, meet my aunt Ida." I gestured to the ghost beside me. "Ida, this is Detective White. You will not be *pranking* him under my roof, do you understand?"

Callie walked past Logan, then sat on the sofa, observing us with an amused expression.

Logan stepped closer to me, squinting his eyes at the space to my right. After a moment, he shook his head. "It's no good, I can't see her." He looked to me. "So this is the ghost who . . . possessed you when Ike attacked you in the woods?"

"Only after the dark magic possessed her," Ida grumbled as I nodded.

Spooky trotted into the room just ahead of Luna, who was drying her hands on a kitchen towel. "Now that that's all cleared up, we should get to planning." She looked to Logan. "While I appreciate you covering up my aunt's antics earlier, you should probably go. We need to speak with her about what the next few days might hold for Adelaide."

Logan squinted his eyes in Ida's direction one last time, then his shoulders slumped. "All right," he looked to me. "I'll pick you up in the morning?"

"What's happening in the morning?" Luna interrupted, moving to sit next to Callie on the sofa.

"Investigation stuff," I explained. "No more questions."

Logan took one look at Luna's determined expression and edged toward the door. "Good luck, Addy. Thanks for dinner, and remember what we talked about."

I waved him off. "Get out of here before Luna explodes."

He quickly let himself outside.

I held up a hand to halt Luna's protests while I waited to hear Logan's car door open and shut. Once his engine started, I lowered my hand and looked at both of my sisters. "I know you're both as nosy as me and dying to know what's going on, but Logan made me promise not to tell. He thinks he's in trouble from the last investigation, and I'm not going to risk his job just because you're curious."

Luna's expression darkened for just a moment, then she relaxed. "Alright, fine, I understand and I don't want Logan's career endangered. We have more important things to worry about regardless." She looked to Ida. "You were alive for several Halloweens after you came into your powers. Tell us everything."

Ida looked pleadingly to Callie. "You're the fun one, tell them we shouldn't waste my few solid nights on this earth with talk."

Callie held up her hands as she leaned back against the sofa cushions. "I may be the fun one, but I'm also the youngest. I know how to pick my battles."

Ida looked down at Spooky as he slunk closer. "You feel for me, don't you, old buddy?" She stared at the cat for a moment, then her expression fell. "Are you sure?" she asked.

I glanced at Spooky, then back to Ida. "Is he talking to you?"

She gave me worried eyes. "I can catch a few words here and there, just like you. Why didn't you tell me there was a necromancer after you?"

"Is it relevant?" I asked.

She tilted her head. "Let's see, necromancers get their power from ghosts and other spirits. Ghosts and other spirits become more powerful around Halloween."

I hadn't thought of that. The necromancer would be more powerful now than ever. I took a deep breath, feeling like I might pass out. "The dark magic and the necromancer are both coming for me within the next few days, aren't they?"

Ida nodded, then looked to Luna. "You're right. Having a necromancer around changes things. We definitely have to spend tonight coming up with a plan. I thought I could protect Addy. I forced the dark magic out of her before, but a necromancer might be able to control me." She turned back to me. "I'm going with you to the scene of the crime tomorrow. We have to make sure it's not connected to the necromancer."

My knees felt like they might give out, so I slumped into the nearest chair. "You were eavesdropping in the bedroom, weren't you?"

Ida floated around to face me, letting the coffee table bisect her legs. "Don't worry, you didn't tell anyone, so you didn't break your promise."

I buried my head in my hands. "Halloween just became my absolute least favorite holiday."

"Mine too," Callie muttered. "I had a really good costume picked out too."

"A container of french fries is not a really good costume," Ida said.

"Hey," Callie whined, "it's only fun when you spy on Addy."

I lifted my head to watch them, but I wasn't really listening. My mind was reeling with all of the things that could go wrong. A good amount of tourists always filtered into Twilight Hollow for Halloween. The town had built a festival around the holiday to drum up business.

It was always a good time of year for the cafe, but now the extra people in town just made extra murder suspects. How could Logan and I be expected to unmask a killer when in two more nights, *everyone* would be wearing masks?

CHAPTER SIX

The next morning I stood in Alison Walker's living room, staring down at the space where she'd been killed. Ida had floated off to search for signs of other spirits. While I had been the one to discover two other murder victims, this was somehow worse, even though the body was gone. The first victim I had seen was stabbed by his own father, a crime of frustration and passion. The second was pushed off a hiking trail by her employee, a crime of resentment and greed. Alison's murder was neither of those things. It was calculated and cold. Ritualistic.

Logan stood quietly behind me, letting me take in the scene.

I noted an end table knocked over by the struggle, fragments of the shattered lamp still littering the wood floor. The books Logan had mentioned lined a nearby bookshelf, all common texts on witchcraft you could buy at any bookstore. Any free space in the living room was taken over by crystals. I didn't check behind the curtains at my back, but I was pretty sure I'd find crystals and other trinkets on the windowsills too. I tugged down the sleeves of my lavender sweater, but its warmth couldn't touch the cold snaking down my spine.

I knew I was stalling, not wanting to look down, but since I didn't see any ghosts around, it was the only thing left for me to do.

I forced my gaze downward, glancing over the symbols scrawled in blood. I could easily picture where her body had been because the symbols would have surrounded it.

"Do you recognize the markings?" Logan asked.

I startled, then quickly shook my head. "No, but Luna or my cousin Amber might. They look like runes, but that's not my forte."

"It's the Celtic Ogham," he explained.

I turned to him. "Why ask if you already knew?"

He lowered his chin, draping a lock of short black hair toward one eye. "You might have seen them as something else. I didn't want to change your thoughts. While we know where the runes come from, we have no idea what it means."

I pulled my phone out of my back pocket, turning

back to the markings. I had to just think of them as markings, not blood. A puzzle, not a murder.

"What are you doing?" Logan stepped up to my side, reaching for the phone.

I stepped away, taking pictures of the blood. "I'm not going to be able to remember all of this, and I may need to refer back to them. I won't show anyone."

He sighed and let his hand fall. "So do you think she was a real witch?"

I shrugged, then put my phone back in my pocket. "If I would have met her when she was alive I could have told you, but there's no way for me to know that now unless her ghost comes around."

"And there's no sign of her?"

I closed my eyes, glad to shut out the bloody scene, then focused my senses on my surroundings. I let out a long breath. "I should have brought Spooky. Maybe he would have noticed something I'm not seeing."

"You couldn't guarantee that he wouldn't touch anything, and you have Ida."

That had been the argument before we left, whether or not we would bring the cat. I hadn't pushed too hard since Spooky wasn't talking to me anyways, but now I wished I had. Ida might be a ghost, but she was still a human teenager in many ways. At least she could talk to Spooky. Bringing me here was useless. I didn't know anything about murder investigations nor the Celtic Ogham.

I shook my head. "I'm sorry, Logan, I don't know if I'm going to be any help here."

He forced a smile, though it didn't nearly reach his dark eyes. "I appreciate you trying regardless. We're still looking for your necromancer. If this was him . . . Addy, is there any danger of this happening to you? If Allison was a real witch—"

I shivered, thinking about my close call with the necromancer in the woods. I looked back down at the blood. "I'll be fine. My sisters are staying with me until after Halloween, and I can call my mom and cousin Amber if things go south."

"Your cousin is still in town?"

Now that I'd gotten over the hurdle of looking at the blood, I couldn't seem to look away. My mind wanted to make sense of it all. "She's staying until we figure out what the dark magic wants with me."

Logan stepped closer to me, looking down at the blood. "I'll take you home. You can let me know if you think of anything later."

We both turned at the sound of a car door shutting out front.

Logan hurried toward the window, peeked past one edge of the curtain, then cursed. He glanced back like he was deciding what to do with me. "Someone is here. Maybe the boyfriend."

"Boyfriend?" I questioned.

"According to her parents, Alison had a new boyfriend. Bradley Maxwell. We've been trying to locate him. If he asks, you're my partner."

I heard footsteps outside, then someone knocked on the door.

Logan was already pulling out his badge as he went to answer it. I waited near the blood stains as Logan explained who he was and what had happened.

The frantic questioning that ensued made me feel sick. I didn't envy Logan his job one bit. Finally, he stepped away from the door and the man, presumably Bradley, came inside.

I took in chin length blond hair, wide brown eyes, and a scruffy face. He was dressed like he'd been out hiking or camping. None of these traits were the most prominent thing about him. No, what stood out couldn't be seen with the naked eye.

Alison's new boyfriend was a warlock. Some magical families passed down powers from mother to daughter. Others went from fathers to sons. The latter were warlocks.

His continued stare told me he recognized me for what I was too, then he noticed the blood. His eyes went wide, horrified. "Alison," he gasped.

I stepped aside. He shouldn't have to look at the blood, but I had a feeling Logan wanted to gauge his reaction to it.

It only took a few seconds though for me to be sure this man had nothing to do with the crime. His face was white as a sheet, and he couldn't tear his eyes away from the symbols in the blood. "Who did this?" he gasped.

He swayed on his feet and I rushed forward to help him onto the clean sofa.

"My phone went dead while I was camping. I charged it and called her this morning, but it went straight to voicemail. I assumed she had let it die." He shook his head over and over, still staring at the blood. "She was always letting her phone . . . die."

Logan remained by the door, watching Bradley's reaction.

I lowered myself onto the sofa. "Bradley, I'm going to ask you something a bit strange. Was Alison a real witch?"

He whipped wide eyes to me, then darted his gaze to Logan.

"It's okay," I soothed. "He knows about . . . things."

Logan stared at me, and I was pretty sure he was starting to comprehend what I had discovered about Bradley. Ida popped up next to Logan, and judging by her expression she had been listening for a while.

Not noticing her, Bradley turned his attention back to me. "No, she wasn't a real witch, and she didn't know what I am. I—" His voice cracked as he looked back to the blood. "I don't understand why someone would do this to her."

Logan stepped in front of Bradley, blocking his view of the blood. "Mr. Maxwell, am I to understand that you *are* a real witch?"

"Warlock," Bradley and I said in unison.

Still out of Bradley's line of sight, Ida glared at the mention of the word.

Logan seemed unsure of what to say, and it was clear he wanted to ask me a million questions, but not in front of the possible suspect. Finally, he pulled the notebook out of his coat pocket. "I have a few questions for you, Mr. Maxwell. We can speak outside if it's easier."

I watched Bradley's throat bob as he gulped. "You mean at the police station? Am I a suspect?"

"No, not yet." Logan looked to me.

It dawned on me that if Logan took Bradley to the station, I couldn't be present for the questioning. I stood. "Let's go outside."

Bradley stood, took one last long look at the blood, then led the way outside. Ida popped out of view before he could see her.

A weight lifted off of my shoulders once we were

out of the house, away from the blood. I never wanted to see a scene like that again, but I had a feeling I'd be seeing it every time I closed my eyes in the near future. Watching Bradley's haunted expression, I imagined he'd be seeing it too. It seemed almost wrong to have the sun shining cheerfully overhead, warming the chill air.

Logan lifted his pen and notebook. "How long have you and Miss Walker been seeing each other?"

Bradley shook his head, wiping a few stray tears from his eyes. "Not long. We met about two months ago through a mutual friend. We had only been officially dating a few weeks."

"Do you know if Miss Walker had any enemies?" Logan asked. "Had she felt like anyone was watching her?"

Bradley shook his head again. "None that she had ever mentioned. She seemed happy. Things were going well."

"Did she have a coven?" I interrupted.

Bradley's spine went stiff. He glanced around the empty street. We could hear children laughing in the distance, but none were near. He turned back to me. "She had a few friends she practiced with. I can give you their names, but I don't think any of them did this to her. No one we know would have done this to her."

"But you've only known her a couple months,"

Logan interjected. "You don't know everyone she knew."

Bradley's shoulders slumped. "You're right, I didn't think about that."

"Back to this coven," Logan pressed on. "Were any of them *real* witches?"

Bradley shook his head. "You're tripping me out, man. You're a mundane. How do you know about us?"

"Addy told me." He gestured in my direction.

"But you believed her? I told one of my girlfriends in the past, but even when I proved it to her, she just wouldn't believe. That's why I wanted to date someone who at least believed in magic. If I eventually told her, she might actually believe me and be cool with it."

It made sense. I wondered why I had never thought of it. Although in general it seemed like more women related to witchcraft than men. If I had used a belief in witchcraft as a prerequisite, my dating pool would have been quite small indeed. Of course, if I had done that, I might not be facing such a sticky situation with Max.

Bradley was looking back and forth between the two of us. "Who do you think did this? Those symbols —this was some sort of ritual. But anyone with actual magic would have known that Alison didn't have any."

"We don't know yet," Logan answered. "But we will find out." He looked to me. "Can you think of any other questions before I take him in for his official statement?"

I shook my head. "I don't think he knows any more than us at this point. I think we should start with Alison's coven. Her close friends might know more than a new boyfriend." I bobbed one shoulder in a half shrug at Bradley. "No offense."

Bradley glanced at the house, then down at his hiking boots. "None taken. Maybe I didn't know Alison as well as I thought. Maybe she had an enemy, or a stalker. Some other mundane who's into witchcraft."

"I'll need you to give an official statement down at the station," Logan explained.

Bradley nodded, his eyes not focusing on anything. "Should I go with you now?"

Logan glanced at me. He had promised my sisters he wouldn't leave me alone, so he needed to take me home before he could bring Bradley to the station. "I'll trust you to meet me there. I just need a few minutes to take Ms. O'Shea home."

Bradley's eyes finally seemed to focus on me. "You mean you're not a cop?"

I wrinkled my nose. "Think of me as a consultant."

He watched me for a moment. "I get it, I won't mention you in my statement. But please let me know if you learn anything about this—" he hesitated. "My brother and I moved to Wickenburg three months ago. It's nice to know . . . " he glanced at Logan, "*people*."

"I'll be in touch," I assured.

Not that I needed any more magic in my life, but knowing the warlocks the next town over was the smart thing to do. The dark magic had come from somewhere, and it was quite the coincidence that it showed up around the time the brothers moved to the area.

Keep your potential enemies close, or something like that.

CHAPTER SEVEN

Luna, Ida, and Spooky were waiting for me when Logan dropped me off just ahead of the storm moving in. Ida had found the car ride boring and decided to jump ahead. I had barely managed to shut my front door when the questions began.

"Was she a real witch?" Luna asked from her perch on my white sofa. She had changed into a deep purple sweater that made her auburn hair look even richer. Dark wash jeans and warm socks completed her look. She really had cleared her calendar for me if she wasn't dressed for the office.

I looked to Ida. "You didn't tell her?"

She shrugged. "I didn't know. I thought you might have figured something out that you weren't saying in front of the detective."

Since Ida was hovering over the nearest chair, I slumped down onto the sofa beside Luna. Spooky hopped into my lap and stared at me, as if wanting an answer to Luna's question.

I shook my head and leaned back against the couch cushion. "You know I have no way to be sure of that, but no I don't think she was. We met her new boyfriend. He's a warlock, and claims the victim was a mundane."

Luna rubbed a hand across her forehead. "Ida mentioned the warlock. Do you think he killed her?"

I wrinkled my brow. Warlocks had a bad reputation. They weren't all bad, of course, but it paid to be cautious. "I don't think he did. He seemed genuinely shocked and upset. He has a brother though, and they both moved to Wickenburg around the time the dark magic first showed up." I sighed. "I shouldn't be telling you any of this. I promised Logan."

"You didn't tell us any details," Luna assured. "And there was no way you could *not* tell us about the warlocks."

Ida floated past the coffee table to hover before me. "That's too big of a coincidence to ignore. Warlocks are bad news. You should tell the detective to make the boyfriend a suspect. If they summoned the dark magic—"

I sighed. "If I decide Bradley and his brother are

involved in the murder, I'll tell Logan, but I don't want him involved with anything concerning the dark magic if I have a choice."

I petted Spooky, deep in thought. The warlocks might be a problem, but I needed to focus on the murder, which meant focusing on Alison's coven. Logan was going to call me as soon as he got a hold of one of them to question.

My cellphone buzzed in my pocket. Assuming it was Logan, I pulled it out to check, but it was a text from Evie.

I groaned, then lowered my phone to my lap next to Spooky.

"What is it?" Luna asked.

I really needed to start keeping a calendar. I was forgetting too many things. "Maura Wimbledon stopped by the cafe to remind me about the special menu I promised for the festival."

"Addy," Luna lectured, "why would you make such plans *now* of all times?"

"I told her I'd do this months ago! I completely forgot. It's no big deal. I'll just bake everything and Evie and Richie can run the cafe."

A knock on the door nearly made me scream. "What is it now?" I huffed, setting Spooky aside before getting up from the couch.

Ida and Luna watched silently as I opened the door.

Max stood outside with a thermos and a bottle of Gatorade. He gave me a hesitant half-smile, like he wasn't sure if he would be welcome. "When Evie said you weren't coming in I worried your migraine had gotten worse. I thought I'd bring you some soup and hydration."

Oh this poor, sweet man, I thought. If he only knew the truth. "Luna already came back to take care of me," I explained. "It's nothing major."

I debated my options. Send the handsome veterinarian bearing food away, maybe away forever, or invite him in and risk him seeing something he shouldn't see.

I stepped back and opened the door further. Other than visiting a crime scene, it had been a quiet morning. A few minutes shouldn't hurt.

Max's smile was more genuine as he stepped inside. I had a feeling this was more than a simple visit. This was him trying to figure out if I actually wanted him around, or if he should back off.

"I'll make us all some coffee," Luna said as I shut the door. She took the thermos and drink from Max with a warm smile, then went into the kitchen, leaving Ida behind.

I did my best to not look at the ghost, but it was an

effort as she watched us with a mischievous grin. I motioned for Max to take a seat on the sofa, and once his back was turned I made a gesture of slitting my finger across my throat at Ida.

She rolled her eyes, then turned and floated after Luna into the kitchen. Hopefully now she would behave herself.

Spooky was already up in Max's lap by the time I sat beside him. "So, no appointments today?"

"Not until this afternoon," he explained, settling against the couch cushions. "I'm not even sure if you like soup, or if that's the right thing for a migraine. And it's probably not as good as anything you would make."

"Oh it could taste like cardboard and I would still appreciate it. No one ever cooks for me."

He pet Spooky absentmindedly. "Duly noted. The next date we have, I'm cooking you dinner—" he hesitated. "That is, if there's going to be a next date."

It seemed my instincts were correct. This wasn't just a casual visit. My phone buzzed in my pocket, but I chose to ignore it. I leaned forward and took his hand. "Of course there's going to be a next date. I'm sorry I've been flaky lately. I've just been really stressed."

His friendly brown eyes were filled with concern. "With the cafe, or is it something else?"

I bit my tongue. I wanted nothing more than to tell him the truth. It would make things so much easier. If he ran, at least I would know now and wouldn't have to experience it further down the road when it would hurt more. I thought about Bradley and fully understood why he would choose to date someone already interested in witchcraft. If he told Alison the truth, she probably wouldn't have run.

"Just the cafe," I sighed, chickening out. "I'm having trouble keeping up with everything, and now Maura just reminded me I had promised a special menu for the festival."

"Ah, the festival," he replied, easily accepting my answer. "I've been hearing a lot about it."

"It's a big moneymaker for the town," I grinned, "and the cafe. I just don't know how I'm going to get all of the baking done in time. I already have Richie and Evie covering for me."

Max shifted a little closer to me. "Can I help? I'll admit I know nothing about baking, but I can follow orders."

It was a thought. Goddess knew I wouldn't be getting any help from my sisters. "Let me think about it. If anything, I might rely on you for some ingredient runs."

He squeezed my hand. "Consider me at your disposal."

As if on cue, Luna returned from the kitchen carrying a tray with three cups of coffee and a saucer of cream. She sat the tray on the table, then lowered herself onto the adjacent chair. "Not as good as what Addy makes, but I'm sure it will do." She gestured to the three steaming mugs.

I reached for one of the mugs. "All you have to do is pour grounds and hot water into the French press. Nothing special." I was grateful Ida hadn't returned with her. Maybe we could actually have a nice cup of coffee with Max, then send him off with none of us the worse for wear.

I sipped the coffee, and Luna was right. It wasn't as good as mine. Imbuing coffee with magic was like second nature to me. I could make it the exact same way as Luna, but mine would always come out better.

Max sipped from his mug, but didn't comment. I wondered if he could tell the difference.

I settled in a little closer to him as we fell into easy conversation. The conversation was always easy with him, maybe because we weren't discussing life or death matters. It was nice talking about the day to day, pretending to be normal. Only Max wasn't pretending. He was normal. Could I really bring him into my crazy world?

Before I knew it we had finished our coffees and nearly an hour had passed. I estimated that I had only heard half of the actual conversation. I opened my mouth to speak, then got interrupted by another knock on the door. I sincerely hoped it was Callie, because I wasn't sure who else might show up.

Before Luna could rise from her seat I had already set my mug aside and went to answer the door. A gust of rain scented air came in as I opened it, revealing Logan standing outside.

I stared at him. He'd had a pretty good excuse for his presence last night, but what the hell was I supposed to tell Max now?

"Don't just stare at me," he chided, pushing his hair back from his face. "I sent you a text that I was coming back by to get you. We found—" he finally looked past me, spotting Max and Luna. "Sorry, I didn't know you had company."

Which wasn't true, he knew Luna was here at least. I quickly debated my options. I could send him away, but I was pretty sure the damage was already done, and if he had gotten a hold of one of Alison's coven members, I wanted to be there for the questioning.

Logan swept past me inside, offering Max his hand. Max stood as they shook.

"Sorry to interrupt your visit," Logan said. "Addy is helping out my sister. She wants to open a cafe in Wickenburg."

Max's brow furrowed, like he didn't quite believe the lie. "She hadn't mentioned that." His eyes flicked to me. "I just stopped by because I knew she wasn't feeling well and I wanted to bring her some soup."

Logan froze for a heartbeat, probably realizing he'd chosen the wrong lie. But I couldn't really blame him, there were too many to keep up with.

"I forgot to cancel," I explained to both men. "But I'm not feeling too bad now, I guess I could still meet with her." I gave Max an apologetic shrug.

Luna watched the entire exchange with an uncomfortable expression.

Max looked at each of us, finally settling on me. "I guess I should go then."

The urge to tell him the truth about everything welled up in me once more. I hated lying. I needed to tell him. I felt so agitated by the situation that it was like bugs crawling all over my skin.

Max moved past me toward the door.

"Make me dinner tonight!" I blurted.

He slowly turned toward me. "Tonight?"

I bit the inside of my cheek and nodded.

He gave me a small smile. "It's a date then. My place at seven?"

I nodded again. "Sounds perfect."

His smile broadened. He waved to Luna and Logan, then went for the door.

I stood stiffly in the middle of my living room until he was gone.

Once we heard his car door shut outside, Luna whirled on me. "What the hell was that? You can't go to his house tonight. Halloween is tomorrow!"

I crossed my arms. "He knew we were lying. I couldn't just let him leave."

Logan watched us both. "Not that I don't *love* being here for this, but I have a murder to solve. Can you two work this out later?"

Luna looked like she might hex him then and there, but she bit her tongue. "Fine, take care of Addy, and I'll be here waiting for her when she gets back." She gave me a pointed look. "Because she *will* be coming back."

I rolled my eyes. "Yes, mother. By the way, how did you get rid of Ida?"

She slumped back down into her seat. "I convinced her it would be fun to go play a trick on Callie."

I chuckled. "Good one, I'll have to remember it. At least until Halloween is over."

She looked up at me from her seat. "Be careful, Addy."

My smile wilted. I knew it was stupid of me to make a date with Max, but I had to live my life, didn't I?

"I'll try," I said. I would have liked to give her a guarantee, but I already had enough lies in my life.

CHAPTER EIGHT

A few minutes later and I was engulfed in the silence of Logan's car as we wove our way through my neighborhood. While the interior was already warm from his arrival, he still turned up the heat.

I shucked my wool coat then re-fastened my seatbelt. Once I was settled, Spooky situated himself on my lap. I didn't care if people looked at me weird for carrying around a cat. If there was a chance having him around could somehow help, I'd take it.

Logan took the first turn that would lead us toward the highway. "Maybe you should just tell your boyfriend the truth."

I glanced at him, but he kept his eyes on the road. Storm clouds thickened overhead. I guessed the rain would hit us before we reached Wickenburg. "You know why I can't, and he's not my boyfriend. Do you even have a sister?"

"No, and I don't know why you can't tell him. You told me. That worked out fine."

I shook my head. "You believed me pretty easily, but most people aren't wired that way. Believing in magic is all fun and games until a witch gets possessed by dark magic and tries to kill you."

He smirked as he slowed to take another turn. "You're going to have to tell him eventually."

I settled back into my seat. "I know. I think I'm going to tell him tonight."

He finally glanced at me, then whipped his eyes back to the road. "Then why argue with me if you were already planning on telling him?"

"I don't like being told what to do." The first raindrops hit the windshield as we exited onto the highway. "So where are we going?"

He glanced at me again. "Alison's coven agreed to meet us at a local bookshop. One of them owns it."

"You sure arranged that quickly."

"The bookshop owner was the first to answer her phone," he explained. "Her name is Meagan Reed. She agreed to gather the others."

"How many?"

He sped up as we hit the highway. Raindrops thundered on the windshield, swept away at high speed by the wipers. "Three. So there were four of them in the coven before Alison was killed."

I snorted.

"What is it?" he sighed.

"You need five witches to make a coven. You can have more than that, but never less."

His fingers flexed on the steering wheel. "We've already established that they aren't real witches."

I shrugged. "Alison wasn't a real witch, at least according to Bradley. The others are yet to be determined. How did it go with Bradley at the station, by the way?"

"Standard. He was out camping when Alison was killed, though he didn't buy a permit so we're still trying to confirm his alibi."

I watched his face, but he gave nothing away. "I don't think he killed her."

He flashed me a quick grin. "Yet to be determined. Now tell me about warlocks."

I watched the road, considering my answer as he changed lanes to go around a semi. "Not much to tell. They're basically male witches, but they do have a bad reputation." I shrugged. "I don't know what the difference is. I guess power corrupts, and maybe men are more susceptible."

"I'll try not to take offense to that."

"Take whatever offense you want, it is what it is."

He laughed. "If you say so. How many warlocks have you known?"

"None."

"Then how do you know they're all bad?"

I rolled my eyes at him. "I didn't say they were all bad, just that they have a bad reputation." I watched him for a moment. "You're just dying to pull out your little notebook and ask me more, aren't you?"

"Maybe, but since I'm driving, how about you just entertain me with any stories you've heard about warlocks. You never know what might end up being important."

I settled back against my seat, petting Spooky as I searched my memories. In truth, I knew few specific stories about warlocks. It was always just more a general warning, my mother or cousin Amber telling me that if I ever met a warlock to run the other way. I'd tell Logan whatever I could though. It felt nice to share with someone, and he was right. The more prepared we were to deal with Bradley and his brother, the better.

I HAD RUN out of warlock stories by the time Logan took the exit toward Wickenburg. Soon enough we were driving down city streets lined with restaurants and bars. If Meagan's bookstore was in this area, she must do good business. I imagined the rent was astronomical. I had briefly considered opening the Toasty Bean in Wickenburg instead of Twilight Hollow, but the rent was a bit too rich for my taste.

Logan read the addresses on the sidewalk curb as he slowed the car, then parallel parked on the street. The rain had lightened to a slight drizzle, which was fortunate since I had forgotten an umbrella.

I glanced around the surrounding shops and restaurants, quickly spotting our destination, *Divine Goddess Bookstore*.

We both exited the car and I carried Spooky as we walked in silence toward the crosswalk. The streets were busy, several people already in costume even though it wasn't Halloween yet. Excited energy filled the air. Young, carefree people were looking forward to a night of fun. While here I was just worried about surviving it.

The crosswalk light turned green and we started walking.

Logan leaned near my shoulder as we reached the sidewalk on the other side. "If they're not real witches, you'll need to let me take the lead."

"Of course," I said, using my free hand to tuck a

damp red curl behind my ear, only to have a chilly gust of air tug it free again.

I looked up at the bookstore's purple and silver sign. Not long ago, I would have searched for some new books to buy. Not that any of the mundane books had ever helped with my powers. I'd simply had to come into them on my own, even though that occurred much later in my life than was normal.

Logan opened the door for me with a jingle of little silver bells on the handle.

I stepped inside, inhaling deeply. I loved the smell of books, and the scent of the vanilla candle near the entry only added to the appeal. I set Spooky down to investigate.

Past the first few shelves were stands of other witchy trinkets. Miniature cauldrons for burning incense, crystals, candles of every color, you name it. Most of them would serve little purpose for me, but my fingers still itched to buy things. I loved a nice crystal as much as the next girl.

There was an area for complimentary coffee near the register with three small round tables.

Two young women were seated at one of the tables, and a third stood behind the register. I assumed the third woman was Meagan. She had hair as curly as mine, but it was platinum blonde. I guessed she was around my age too. She wore a black velvet top with delicate silver jewelry.

Her blue eyes narrowed warily. "Are you the detectives?"

Logan flashed his badge. "I appreciate you meeting with us, Ms. Reed."

The other two women at the table stood, leaving half empty disposable coffee cups behind. The shorter of the two with chin length black hair and large dark eyes introduced herself as Nina, and the other, a tall girl with mousy hair down to her waist quietly announced that her name was Jodi. Both of them wore simple clothing and only a few small pieces of jewelry, not what you would think of as typical witch attire. With her oversized flannel and loose jeans, Jodi looked about fifteen years old, though I guessed she was actually in her mid-twenties.

Meagan came around the counter to stand near the other two girls. As soon as she did they seemed more confident, like she would protect them. "What happened to Alison?" she asked.

"You three should probably sit down," Logan said, gesturing to their vacated seats.

He sat down with them, but didn't tell me what to do, so I took the opportunity to wander. I really didn't want to see their faces when they heard that their friend was dead. If one of them didn't express the shock and horror expected, I trusted Logan to catch it. I didn't need to see. I could come back for the actual questioning.

I walked through rows of books, perusing the titles. A few of them I recognized because the same ones were on Alison's shelves. None of the girls were actually witches, which only emphasized the fact that I wouldn't be any help in the investigation. The murderer was probably some mundane whack-job.

I had started to reach for a gorgeous hunk of amethyst when one of the girls started crying. I froze mid-motion, my shoulders stiffening as I imagined myself in her position.

I closed my outstretched hand into a fist. Suddenly I didn't give a damn if the murderer was a mundane. I wanted to nail them to a wall regardless.

I made my way back to the table.

Nina was the one weeping. Jodi hung her head, hiding her face with that long hair. But Meagan— Meagan looked *pissed*. I had a feeling that when we nailed the murderer to the wall, she would gladly be there handing us a hammer.

I pulled out a chair from an adjacent table and turned it to face the others. I sat and crossed my arms, listening as Meagan explained that she had seen Alison the previous morning, and that everything had seemed fine.

She shook her head, raking thin fingers through her curls and making them frizz. "Who would do this? I don't understand."

I watched the girls as Logan went through the normal questions. Did Alison have any enemies? Did she feel like anyone was watching her? Their answers were the same as Bradley's. He even asked them about the Celtic Ogham, though he didn't reveal how it was related to the murder.

"There was one weird thing," Jodi cut in, piquing my interest. "Bradley's brother Damon had a small party about a week ago. All of us went. There was a really creepy guy there. Tall and thin with dark hair. He gave me a weird vibe."

"Did he talk to Alison at all?" I asked.

She nodded. "He talked to all of us, but after he shook our hands he seemed to lose interest."

I leaned back in my seat, considering her words. Some witches and warlocks could read people through touch. My mom and sisters all could to varying degrees. It was a lot to assume though on one girl's weird vibes.

"Did you get his name?" Logan asked.

Jodi shook her head. "No, but maybe Bradley knows, or maybe his brother, Damon."

Another mention of the brother had me really

wanting to meet him. Maybe he would prove more interesting than Bradley.

Spooky hopped up onto my lap, startling me.

Nina gasped, holding a hand to her chest. "Is that your cat?"

I patted Spooky's head. "Sorry about him. He doesn't like being left at home."

Meagan watched me with narrowed eyes, but didn't comment.

"Back to the party," Logan interjected. "Did anything else strange happen?"

I tuned out their words, wondering about the man at the party. Tall, thin, with dark hair. It could be any number of people, but the description did fit the necromancer. Runes painted in blood fit what a necromancer might do. He would have known that Alison wasn't a real witch, but maybe it didn't matter. Maybe he just needed a sacrifice and appreciated the irony.

Or maybe he knew I was friends with a homicide detective who might bring me in on the case.

"Addy," Logan was saying, and I realized it wasn't the first time he'd said my name. He stood. "Let's go."

I saw his business card on the table. The three girls watched us with hollow eyes.

"Call us if you think of anything else," Logan told the girls.

I gathered Spooky up and stood. "I'm sorry for your

loss." I met Meagan's defiant eyes and wondered what she was going to do after we left. Would she try to find the killer herself?

I hoped not. If the killer was the necromancer, she wouldn't stand a chance. We would just have to find him before she could.

With a final wave to the girls we left the bookstore and headed toward Logan's car.

"So what do you think?" he asked as we walked down the sidewalk.

I lowered my voice, moving close to his shoulder. "None of them are real witches. And I'm worried Meagan might try to take things into her own hands."

Logan bobbed his head, keeping his eyes on the passersby. "Agreed. I'm going to question Bradley about the party and see if he knows the man who talked to the girls. And I'll get his brother's information. I assume you want to be present to meet the other Mr. Maxwell?"

"I do, as long as it's not tonight."

We stopped at the crosswalk. "Ah yes, the big date. So are you really going to tell him?"

I gnawed my lower lip, clutching Spooky tightly as the light turned green and we started walking. "I think I have to. He knows I'm lying to him about something."

We reached Logan's car. He paused with his hand on the driver's side door to look over the roof at me. "I guess all I can say is good luck. I hope you still have a boyfriend come morning."

"He's not my boyfriend," I muttered as I opened the passenger side door with my free hand.

And after tonight, he might never be.

CHAPTER NINE

I was ten minutes late for my date. Ten extra minutes spent arguing with Luna and Callie, added to the hours before. Since I was going no matter what they said, we had finally settled on Luna and Callie dropping me off and waiting at a nearby pet-friendly bar with Spooky. That part was fine, the part I didn't like was that Ida would be joining me on my date. If any spirits showed up, she'd fetch my sisters.

Hopefully it wouldn't come to that. I hadn't seen any other spirits since Ida's arrival, so maybe our worries were for nothing.

She hovered next to me as I knocked on the door of the two-story Victorian Max had inherited from his family. He lived on the opposite side of town from me, hence my sisters not just waiting at home.

"This house is oddly familiar to me," Ida muttered.

Ignoring her, I huddled in my coat, lifting my hand to knock again. I would've been warmer in something other than tight jeans and a white long-sleeved v-neck beneath the coat, but I wanted to look nice. Maybe if Max took the news badly I could distract him with my womanly wiles.

Then again, maybe not. It wasn't every day you found out your romantic interest was a witch.

He answered the door just as I was about to knock again, letting out a wash of warm air. He wore a burgundy plaid button up that suited his brown eyes and lighter brown hair, the latter of which was freshly combed rather than the usual tousled mess. He also wore slacks instead of jeans, another unusual sight.

He'd dressed up for me, just like the previous night. Suddenly I was incredibly nervous. My palms begin to sweat.

"Well, are you coming inside? You must be freezing out there."

I jumped, realizing I'd been gawking at him like an idiot. I hurried inside, ignoring Ida. She had sworn up and down that she would behave herself, and I could only cross my fingers and hope she'd be true to her word.

We walked through the entry room and into the living room, our shoes echoing across the hardwood floors. Though the house was a classic Victorian, Max's decorating style tended more toward log cabin with a cushy sofa and earth tones. I appreciated the decor, even though it seemed a little out of place. It was cozy.

I could smell something cooking in the kitchen. Scratch that, I could smell something *burning*.

I lifted a brow as he took my coat. "Do you maybe want to check on dinner?"

He cursed, finally seeming to notice the smell. He tossed my coat on the sofa and headed toward the kitchen.

Ida appeared at my side. "Your boyfriend can't cook. I guess if he breaks up with you tonight it won't be a total loss."

I scowled at her. "Remember, you promised to behave."

I turned away and followed Max into the kitchen, finding him shoving a baking sheet onto one half of the stovetop before sucking on a burnt finger. The rolls on the pan closely resembled charcoal briquettes.

He turned as he noticed me, giving me an embarrassed shrug. "The rolls are toast, but everything else should be okay."

I moved up beside him and gave him a pat on the shoulder. "It was a valiant effort."

I looked over the rest of what he had done. He didn't have a separate dining area, but the kitchen was large enough to fit a full dining table with six chairs, though I knew he didn't entertain much. The table already had two place settings ready to go, accompanied by a freshly opened bottle of Cabernet and two empty wine glasses.

I approached the table, filled one glass, and sat down, leaning back in my chair. "I'm ready to be wowed."

Max turned back to the stovetop, sliding on oven mitts to lift the covered baking dish opposite the pan of burnt rolls. He brought it to the table, set it on a dish towel, then lifted the lid.

It smelled a heck of a lot better than the rolls. A whole roast chicken surrounded by carrots, mushrooms, and onions. I smelled thyme, basil, and a healthy basting of real butter.

My mouth watered. "And here I thought you couldn't cook."

He went back to the kitchen counter, then returned oven mitt free with a carving knife. "No, I can't bake. And the cooking is limited." Despite his words I could tell he was proud as he carved the chicken.

Once our plates were filled and we both had our wine, we fell into our normal conversation about the Toasty Bean, his vet clinic, and the people in our lives.

The evening wore on without incident. I almost

felt like I was a normal girl on a normal date, though the secret I needed to share with Max felt heavy on my shoulders. Was this about to turn into not a normal date, but our last date?

Once our plates were cleared, we went into the living room with our wine. I had told him that Callie needed to borrow my car, so she offered to drop me off and pick me up, and should be by with Luna around ten. It was already 9:30 and I was running out of time.

"So Max," I began, swirling my half-empty wine glass. "There's something I've been meaning to talk to you about."

He set his wine glass on the coffee table, then gave me his full attention. "Should I be worried?"

I grimaced. "That part is really up to you."

He took my free hand. "I'm listening. I hope you feel comfortable telling me, whatever it is."

My heart thundered in my chest. I had been pretty much forced into telling Logan, but this was different. This time I was making a choice, and more hung in the balance.

"I'm—" A knock sounded on the door. "Dammit, Callie," I muttered. "You're early."

Max patted my knee, then went to answer the door.

I slumped back against the couch cushions, taking a deep swill of wine.

"Hmm," Max said, returning from the entryway. "No one there."

My pulse picked back up. It could have just been kids playing ding dong ditch. Halloween often inspired such activities in the youngsters. But Halloween also inspired ghosts.

"You did hear someone knock, right?"

He watched me for a moment. "No, when you muttered about Callie being here early I assumed you heard your car."

My mouth went dry. I had definitely heard the knock, but Max hadn't.

Wine glass still in hand, I stood. "I need to use the bathroom."

I hurried away before Max could say anything else. The guest bathroom was on the first floor, facing the street. If there was a ghost outside, I should be able to see it through the window.

I reached the bathroom, went inside, then shut and locked the door behind me, placing my glass on the counter. I hadn't thought to set it down before rushing off.

The bathroom was dark save a small nightlight, but I didn't bother with the main lights. If there was someone outside, I wanted to see them before they saw me.

With trembling hands, I opened the small window,

to stare at Ida. I snapped my mouth shut, then shook my head. "Never mind," I laughed. "I was just wondering if you ever figured out why it happened, but that's silly. I'm sure you would have told me if you did."

Max took a cautious step toward me. "Addy—"

I moved forward, placed my hands on either side of his jaw, and kissed him.

He hesitated a moment, then kissed me back.

My mind raced. Ida had looked so frantic. I could sense her hovering near, watching us, but I took my time with the kiss. I didn't want Max to think anything was wrong until I knew what Ida was suddenly so worried about.

When I finally pulled away, I managed a reassuring smile. "I'm going to be busy all day tomorrow baking for the festival, but give me a call when you get a chance?"

He smiled. "I can still pick up ingredients if you need them. I'd offer to help with the baking, but . . . "

I smirked. "Yeah, I saw the rolls. I won't be letting you anywhere near my oven." I gave him another quick kiss. "I shouldn't keep my sisters waiting. Thanks for dinner."

"My pleasure. Any time you don't want to be the one stuck cooking, just let me know. I can cook for your sisters too."

I pulled away. "Don't tell them that, you'll never leave the kitchen again."

His smile fell. "Addy, are you sure nothing is wrong?"

I wanted to scream at Ida. I had finally almost told him, and she had thwarted me.

"I'm really just tired. I promise I'll figure out something with the baking and the cafe soon, and things will go back to normal."

He nodded, but I could tell he didn't fully believe me.

Unfortunately, there was nothing I could do about it in that moment. I fetched my coat from the back of the couch, then headed toward the door with Ida watching me all the while. It seemed to take an eternity to say our final goodbyes, then to walk out the door and down the driveway toward my waiting car. My sisters were in both the front seats with the heat blasting, forcing me into the back, but I hardly thought about it.

As soon as I was inside with Spooky on my lap, Ida appeared in the seat next to me.

I glanced at Luna in the driver's seat. "Let's get moving, I have a lot to tell you guys, and I think Ida has something to tell us right now."

Luna put the car into gear and pulled out onto the dark street, all of us silently waiting for Ida to speak, but she seemed terrified.

Finally, once Max's house was out of sight and we were driving slowly through the next neighborhood, Ida let out a long exhale. "How much do you girls know about my death?"

I blinked at her. It was the last thing I had been expecting her to say. "Not much. Mom has never liked talking about it. We know you died when you were a teenager, and it had something to do with your gifts. We kind of just assumed you went crazy and jumped off a bridge or something."

Her transparent mouth sealed into a grim line at my words. Spooky left my lap and padded across the seat to nuzzle against her arm.

She pet him, though her eyes were focused out the window. She didn't look at any of us as she explained, "I guess I did go crazy, but it was my first boyfriend that pushed me to the edge. He knew what I was, and he pushed me with my gifts more and more. It was only after I died that I learned he was a witch hunter."

I narrowed my eyes at the back of her head. "Ida, witch hunters aren't real. The people killed during the witch trials were mundanes."

Finally, she turned to face me. "They are real, Adelaide. Our ancestors didn't always keep their powers a secret, and some mundanes learned what we really were and they hated us for it."

Callie turned around in her seat to look at both of

us, her eyes wary. "Ida, why are you telling us all of this now?"

Ida looked right at me as she replied, "While Addy was on her date I decided to snoop around her boyfriend's house a little bit. I had found a photo album, but didn't have a chance to look at it because that ghost showed up. But when she sent me off again, I decided to take a look. My old boyfriend, Isaac Howard, was Max's father."

Luna slammed on the brakes. "What!"

My body whipped forward, then I clutched at the back of my suddenly sore neck. "Geez, warn a girl if you're going to do that."

I looked back to Ida. "This has to be some sort of mistake."

She shook her head, unfazed by Luna's screeching halt, unlike the rest of us. "That's why I recognized the house. I only went there once, so I didn't remember at first. When I saved you from that man in the woods, I thought I recognized him. You even called him Ike, but I just couldn't believe that it was Ike Howard, Isaac's brother."

My mouth went dry. Luna hadn't started driving again yet, instead she was staring back at us.

"Ike Howard was your boyfriend's brother?" I asked weakly.

Sympathy flooded her expression as she nodded.

"I'm sorry, Addy. Max is the son of a witch hunter, which means he already knows what you are. He's probably dating you to find proof."

I leaned back in my seat, shocked.

Callie undid her seatbelt, then turned to see me better. "He might not know. Maybe his dad never told him about any of this. It could just be a coincidence."

"You know how I feel about coincidences," I breathed.

Luna eased off the brakes and started heading toward home. "We don't need to jump to any conclusions, and we have a more pressing problem to deal with right now. Let's focus on that, and we'll cautiously look into what Max may or may not know. Ida said a warlock's ghost visited you tonight?"

I knew Bradley getting killed was important, but it was an effort to tear my thoughts away from Max. I weakly explained to my sisters what had happened. Once I was able to get the full story from Bradley, I needed to call Logan.

I sat up a little straighter. And maybe Logan could do a background check on Max. The thought of it felt slimy to me, going behind Max's back in such a way. But if he was actually a witch hunter, I needed to know. I needed to know if he had a history of violence, or anything worse.

I really couldn't picture it, but I had been fooled before.

Spooky left Ida and returned to my lap.

I stared down at him, but my thoughts were so jumbled I could hardly focus.

Danger, Spooky said into my mind.

I paused with my hand mid-pet and stared down at him, willing him to say more. But now that I was focusing, it was like a wall had been slammed up between us.

Bradley had been murdered. Max might be a witch hunter. Could my boyfriend and the murderer be one and the same?

CHAPTER ELEVEN

I wanted nothing more than to go to bed once I got home. I knew no matter what, I'd be baking all morning tomorrow, and I hated functioning on little sleep. I would have liked to wallow in my own problems, but Bradley's problems were bigger.

He had been murdered, after all.

He was waiting outside my front door when we pulled up into the driveway. The headlights cut across his spectral form, making him disappear in places. I'd had to give him directions. Apparently ghosts could track my energy, but they couldn't find my house when I wasn't there. Although that didn't stop them from following me home, so it wasn't like it added any protection.

I was the first one out of the car, holding Spooky

against my chest, appreciating his warmth through the thickness of my coat.

"You know you can just walk through walls now," I said to Bradley as I approached. "You didn't have to wait outside."

He shrugged. "It seemed rude to go in on my own, and it's not like I can get cold anymore."

I heard my sisters getting out of the car behind me, and suddenly Ida was at my side. She looked Bradley up and down. "I know you were a warlock. You better not pull any tricks over the next few days. We may both lose our more solid forms after Halloween, but that doesn't mean I can't kick your butt all the way to the afterlife. I've been hanging onto this realm a lo-ong time."

Bradley frowned. "No offense, but I was just murdered. I'm not really worried about your threats."

"Enough," I said. "Those of us amongst the living are freezing, so let's go inside and figure this out."

Callie and Luna headed quietly toward the door. I hated how quiet they were. I knew they were both thinking about Max, warlocks, and witch hunters. And about how silly and defenseless their sister was.

I stomped into the house after them, setting Spooky down as soon as we were inside. *Danger*, he'd said to me in the car. Yeah, no kidding.

I hung my coat on a wall hook, then slumped down onto the sofa as Callie locked the front door.

Luna headed into the kitchen. "I'll make some tea."

Once Callie, Bradley, and Ida were all gathered around the couch, I sat up a little straighter, looking to Bradley. "Tell me what happened."

He floated toward a chair. "I don't really know. After I met Detective White at the station to give my statement, I called my brother and told him what happened to Alison. We were going to meet at a bar, have a few drinks, but I never made it. I was attacked as soon as I got out of my car."

"In a public parking lot?" I asked.

He nodded. "It was even still light outside. I have no idea what happened."

I stroked my chin in thought.

Callie stepped forward from where she had been leaning her back against the wall. "Your attacker must have been magical. A mundane couldn't pull something like that off."

My stomach turned at my next thought. I gave Bradley a preemptive apologetic smile. "I hate to ask this, but did you see your body? Do you know where it is?"

He nodded. "There was a long period of darkness after I was killed. Once I came to, I was with my body .

. . in the river. My arm got caught on some driftwood, anchoring me to the shore."

I swallowed the lump in my throat. "Do you think you could explain just where it is? I need to call the detective and let him know you're dead."

"I think so," he breathed. "Can you tell my brother too?"

Luna came back into the living room with three steaming mugs on a platter. I smelled lavender and chamomile, so she'd gone for soothing instead of caffeinated. Maybe she actually expected us to get some sleep tonight.

Callie lifted one mug then sat beside me on the couch, looking over at Bradley. "Can't you just tell him yourself? He's a warlock, and it's almost Halloween. He should be able to see you."

Bradley suddenly seemed close to tears. "Imagine you were just killed, and you're the one that has to tell one of your sisters that you were murdered."

Callie audibly gulped. "Yeah, I guess I would delay breaking the news as long as possible, and I'd gladly push the task off on someone else."

Bradley moved his head, stretching his neck from side to side. Obviously just an old habit as his neck would never feel stiff again, or maybe he was just trying to hide the spectral tears now falling down his cheeks.

He shouldn't have been embarrassed. I was impressed he had held it together as long as he had.

I stood. "We are going to figure out who did this to you, Bradley. And I'll have the detective notify your brother. Maybe tomorrow, once you've had some time to process, we can go visit your brother together."

He inhaled deeply, then let out a long breath. "Thank you, I appreciate that."

I went to find my phone in my coat pocket by the door with the intention of calling Logan, only to find I already had a text from him.

Sorry to interrupt your date, but I can't find Bradley.

I stared at the words for a minute, feeling almost guilty to add another murder to Logan's plate. I knew he was stressed about his career as it was.

I selected the text, then hit the call button.

He answered on the first ring. "Are you home, or did I interrupt you?"

"Home, and no you didn't interrupt. Bradley's ghost did that job for you."

He was silent for several seconds. "Say that again?"

"You better get over here if you want to question him. He thinks he can tell you where his body is."

Another moment of silence, then, "Nothing is ever simple, is it?"

"You're the homicide detective. You tell me."

He sighed. "I'll be there in twenty minutes."

IT WAS after eleven by the time I heard Logan's car pull up. I had changed into loose gray sweats and a chunky white fisherman's sweater. If I had to stay awake, I was at least going to be comfortable. I had also whipped up a batch of pumpkin scones and stuck them in the oven as a trial for one of my festival recipes. The plan was to make everything spooky or harvest themed. Donuts with black icing and orange marmalade filling, cream cheese tarts in the shape of ghosts, miniature sweet potato pies, you name it. Maybe I could have gone less complicated with the limited amount of time, but the harvest festival was a showcase of all the restaurants in Twilight Hollow. I was simply too competitive to half-ass things. I could bake some things tonight and some first thing in the morning, then make my sisters deliver them while I prepared more recipes for the lunch rush. I would need more ingredients too, but I'd just have to make do with what I had for tonight.

The oven timer dinged at the same time Logan knocked, so I asked Callie to answer the door while I checked on the scones.

I was sliding the scones onto a cooling rack when Logan walked into the kitchen behind me.

"You're baking at a time like this?"

I slid the last scone onto the rack then turned, leaning my butt against the counter. "I'll be baking all day tomorrow too. I'm supposed to have a whole special menu for the Harvest Festival."

He looked tired. His white shirt beneath his charcoal suit was wrinkled and boasted a highly apparent coffee stain. He noticed me looking at it and lifted a hand to futilely wipe at the stain. "I spilled on the way over here and didn't want to take the time to go home and change. Is Bradley still around?"

I watched as Bradley floated in from the living room, observing Logan. He waved a hand in front of his face. "I mean, I knew he wouldn't be able to see me, but this is just weird."

"He's floating right next to you," I explained to Logan.

Spooky came into the kitchen and hopped up on the counter beside me, his yellow eyes on Bradley.

Logan watched the cat. "Even the cat can see the ghost, can't he." He didn't say it like it was a question, more like he was just disappointed to be the only one in the house who couldn't see the ghost.

Ida floated into the room past Bradley.

I bobbed a hand in her direction, my attention on Logan. "Ida is here now too, just so you know."

Logan rubbed his brow and shook his head. "Too weird." He pulled his little notebook out of his coat pocket, then looked in Bradley's general direction. "We should probably start with your body. If you can tell me where to find it, we'll call in an anonymous tip to the station."

Bradley nodded, then started giving Logan directions while I translated.

Logan seemed distracted, and I had to repeat some of the directions several times. Finally, I paused and moved toward him, placing a hand on his arm. "Are you okay?"

He lowered his notebook and shook his head. For a moment I thought he wouldn't answer, then he said, "I let Bradley leave the station, and he was murdered shortly after. It feels a little bit like my fault."

Bradley placed a spectral hand on Logan's other shoulder. "You couldn't have known, man. And I don't think you could have stopped whatever came for me."

I felt Logan's arm go tense. He looked at me with wide eyes. "Is the ghost touching me? I feel like the ghost is touching me."

I looked to Bradley, who quickly retracted his hand, then to Ida, who shrugged. I turned back to Logan. "Yeah, he touched your shoulder. I'm surprised you felt it, but if you were ever going to sense a ghost, it's the time for it. If you're sensitive enough to sense a touch, you might even notice a bit more tomorrow."

Logan thought about it for a moment, then simply

said, "Interesting. I'm going to run to a payphone to call in an anonymous tip about Bradley, then I'll be back with more questions."

Finding it difficult to resist any longer, I snatched one of my freshly baked scones from the cooling rack and took a bite. "We'll be here," I said with my mouth half-full.

But Logan was already turning away with his eyes scanning the directions he had written in his notebook. He walked out of the kitchen, leaving me alone with Ida and Bradley.

"Will he call my brother soon?" Bradley asked.

I took another bite of my scone before replying, "The police have to find the body first, otherwise Logan should have no way of knowing that you're dead. It would look suspicious if your brother were notified too soon."

I heard Logan go out the front door, then Callie came into the kitchen. Luna had gone upstairs to rest.

Callie raked a hand through her already wild strawberry blonde curls. "Is Logan coming back, or are we good to get some rest?"

I smiled. She looked nearly as bad as Logan with her wrinkled silk top and a drying spot of tea on her jeans. "You rest, I'll wait and translate any more questions he has for Bradley when he gets back."

Callie crossed her tattooed arms and looked

Bradley up and down. "You better behave yourself, warlock. We have a full coven around right now, don't think we won't banish you." She hesitated at Bradley's downtrodden expression. "And sorry you're dead," she added before turning away.

I rubbed my stiff neck as I turned back to the scones, thinking about what I should make next. Even if I made some of the more delicate pastries now, a touch of magic could keep them fresh for the morning. I already knew that I was going to have too much to do, especially with Bradley's murder now on my plate. Maybe I could enlist help from the two ghosts floating in my kitchen.

Spooky cupcakes made by real ghosts. I'd like to see Margo's Cafe on the other side of town top that.

CHAPTER TWELVE

The ghosts had wandered off by the time Logan returned, so Spooky was the only one with me when I went to answer the door, dusting flour off my hands as I walked. I had reached the strange, dreamlike state of being way too tired, where my steps seemed lighter than they were, and Logan's pounding on my door seemed unbelievably loud in the quiet house.

I stopped right in front of the door. Wait, it *was* unbelievably loud. Why was he pounding at my door so incessantly?

I walked to the nearest shelf and grabbed a heavy chunk of quartz crystal, hiding it at my side before returning to the door and opening it.

A man I didn't recognize stood outside. He was tall, probably around six foot with white-blond hair and narrowed pale eyes. I couldn't tell the exact color in the moonlight, and that was all I saw of him as he charged toward me.

"What did you do with my brother, witch!"

I chucked the crystal at his head. It hit him, staggering him backwards. It would have been a stretch for me to have time to slam the door in his face and lock it, so I retreated to my living room, searching for something else to hit him with.

The man stumbled inside, holding one hand over a bloody gash on his forehead.

"Addy!" I heard Callie's voice behind me on the stairs, but I couldn't turn to look as Spooky launched himself at my attacker, claws poised to rake his face.

I snatched up a heavy book, and as the man turned away, shielding himself from Spooky, I slammed it into his jaw.

He fell to the ground, groaning.

Luna and Callie appeared on either side of me as I stood over him with my book, panting and shaken.

"Who the hell is that?" Callie asked.

"Damon!" Bradley rushed through the front door with Ida following close behind.

I stepped back, still clutching the book as Bradley floated down beside the man on the floor, who was now sitting up, clutching his jaw.

"Damon," Bradley repeated more calmly. "Why were you attacking Addy?"

I watched as my attacker regained his senses. Now that I had a moment to look at him, I noticed that he was wearing a suit, like he had just gotten off work, though it was the middle of the night.

He slowly turned toward the sound of Bradley's voice, then gasped and staggered to his feet. "What did these witches do to you?" He aimed a finger at me and my sisters.

Luna had the good sense to slip past him and shut the front door. We really didn't want the neighbors hearing any of this and calling the cops.

Spooky stood in front of me protectively as I crossed my arms and looked Damon up and down. "The other Mr. Maxwell, I presume?"

"Addy is helping me," Bradley explained before Damon could speak. "She's a channeling witch. I was drawn to her after I was killed."

Damon seemed to be struggling to process it all. He stared at Bradley for a moment, then swatted a tear from his eye. "Who did this to you? I didn't hear from you all night after you didn't show up for drinks, so I scried for your location, but the crystal kept pointing to two different places. One location was in the middle of the woods, and the other was here."

"The other location must've been where Bradley's body is," Callie muttered to me and Luna.

Damon whirled on her. "You stay out of this, witch."

Bradley floated between Damon and Callie, facing his brother. "Please, Damon. These witches are trying to find out who killed me. They're working with a detective."

Damon stared through his brother at Callie. "They're witches, we can't trust them."

Bradley floated closer to his brother. "I met Addy before I was killed. She's working with the detective on Alison's murder."

Damon watched his brother for a moment longer, then his shoulders slumped. He turned toward me, observing every aspect of my appearance way too closely. "You would think I would have sensed a channeling witch this close to Wickenburg."

Bradley floated away from his brother to turn toward us. "Damon is a scryer and clairvoyant. He can find anyone or anything."

Callie crossed her arms. "Some clairvoyant if he thought Addy was a murderer."

Luna sighed as she walked past us all toward the sofa. "Clairvoyants get visions from touching objects, and they can't control which visions they get. He saw two different locations for his brother, so I imagine he realized his brother had been separated from his body, and was led to the house of a witch. I don't think we can blame him for his assumptions."

I glared at her as she sat on the couch. "We can blame him for trying to kill me though."

"I think you were the one trying to kill me," Damon said, drawing my attention as he dabbed a finger at the blood on his forehead.

The curse words I was about to fling at him were cut off by another knock on the door.

"It's me," Logan said from outside.

"Who is that?" Damon hissed.

I glared at him as I went to open the door. "The detective trying to solve your brother's murder, just like the rest of us."

I opened the door, stepping aside for Logan to survey the scene.

He hesitated on the threshold. "Addy, what the hell happened?"

I shook my head. "Come inside and we can all have a chat. Did the police find Bradley's body?"

He eyed Damon. "That's something we should discuss in private."

I sighed, gesturing back toward the warlock. "This is Damon Maxwell, Bradley's brother."

Damon stepped up beside me. "Where is my brother's body?"

I didn't think he was going to try to grab me again, but I moved out of reach anyway, which put me further into the house.

Finally, Logan stepped inside next to Damon and shut the door behind him. Instead of answering Damon, he looked at me. "That's what took me so long. I waited to be called in about the body after the station took the anonymous tip."

"And?" Damon pressed.

Logan looked around the room at all of us. "The body couldn't be found. Either it ended up further down the river, or someone moved it. There will be a search, but if we can't find it there will be no investigation beyond missing persons."

"I can find it," Damon said. "I'll scry for it now."

I turned to explain what scrying was to Logan, and it was only then that I realized Ida wasn't in the room.

Then I sensed something else. Something enormous, bone chilling, and powerful. The dark magic had come for me at last.

CHAPTER THIRTEEN

I froze. I knew I should warn everyone, but I couldn't seem to form the words. The dark magic was powerful on a normal day, now it felt massive and all-consuming.

Logan was the first to notice my expression. He eyed me warily. "Addy, what's wrong?"

Luna realized it next. She stood from the couch, glancing around. "It's here, isn't it?"

Damon stepped away from us. "What is that? I sense something ancient."

"Where did Ida go?" Bradley asked, but I didn't have time to answer him.

Green fog snaked into the room from all directions. From the kitchen, from underneath the front door, and down the stairs. It had slipped past my sister's wards like they were nothing.

In the blink of an eye it had filled the entire room. My sisters both rushed toward me, each taking one of my hands while Spooky twined around my legs.

Logan watched us all wide-eyed, unable to see the fog.

I held my sisters' hands, preparing for the magic to try to take me over. Luna started chanting a protection spell. Callie and I joined in. The pressure built until it was almost unbearable. I could barely hear myself chanting. I closed my eyes tightly, trying to concentrate. Then with a loud *pop*, the magic broke, flooding the room.

Wind whipped across my face. I struggled to open my eyes just a crack, spotting Logan trying to make his way toward me and my sisters.

The front door slammed open, banging against the wall. The wind swirled around Damon. He put his hands up defensively, but it swept him up, tossing him in a tornado of green mist out the door. Bradley had disappeared at some point too, but I'd been so focused on protecting myself that I didn't notice.

The door slammed shut. As quickly as it had appeared, the magic was gone.

Logan wiped a sheen of sweat from his brow, then rushed to check the front door. With his hand on the knob, he looked back at the three of us. "It's locked," he panted. "What just happened?"

I blew a lock of hair out of my face, my curls turned to frizzy dandelion fluff by the wind. "I have absolutely no idea."

Callie dropped my hand, wiping her sweaty palms on her jeans. She glanced around the room. "Where did it go? Was it the protection spell? Did it work?"

Luna dropped my other hand and stepped away, smoothing her hair before tugging down her sweater. "It wasn't that type of protection spell and you know it."

Pounding on the door signaled Damon's recovery.

Logan unlocked the door and opened it, but didn't move for Damon to come inside.

Not that it mattered. He glared at us all from outside, his blond hair sticking out in all directions. "I knew you witches were bad news. You're playing with dark magic. I'll find my brother and solve his murder myself."

I started to explain that we didn't summon the dark magic, but he was already walking away.

Logan watched him for a moment, then shut the door and turned to us. "I'm going to need a little more detail about what just happened."

"No time," Luna snapped. "Callie, start repairing the wards. Just because the dark magic was able to break them doesn't mean they aren't still useful to keep other things out." She turned her attention to me. "Take Spooky and see if you can summon Ida. We can only hope the dark magic didn't banish her." Next she turned her attention to Logan. "Your best chance of finding Bradley's body is to work with Damon, and that's not going to happen if you're here with us."

Logan smoothed back his mussed hair, straightened his suit jacket, and looked to me.

With a grunt of annoyance, Luna took Callie's hand and pulled her into the kitchen.

I knelt down to pick up Spooky, but when I held out my hands I realized how badly they were shaking. The thinning of the veil had empowered the dark magic, and it had used that newfound power to break through the wards on the house. It had used its power to . . . get rid of Damon?

Logan knelt in front of me, trapping Spooky between us as he took my trembling hands in his. "Addy, what's going on? One minute we were having a calm conversation, then that wind came."

I gave his hands a squeeze, then pulled away. I was steady enough to lift Spooky into my arms and stand. "It was the dark magic. I thought it was going to try to possess me again, but it left as soon as it tossed Damon outside. I think it banished the ghosts too. I need to find Ida. She might be too weak to reach out to me."

"I'm not too weak," a voice said behind me.

Relief flooded me as I turned to find Ida floating near the sofa.

"The dark magic forced me out," she explained. "It broke your wards, then warded the house against me. It took me a while to break through. Did you banish it?"

Clutching my cat, I gulped, then shook my head.

She floated toward me, her expression intent. "It left on its own?"

I nodded. "As soon as it got rid of Damon."

She stopped in front of me. "You mean it showed up shortly after the warlock arrived, and disappeared once it got rid of him?"

I nodded again. Callie and Luna had both come to the entryway to listen in.

"Addy," Ida began patiently. "You've had four close encounters with the dark magic. The first time when it empowered a ghost to attack you, the next, when Ike Howard was trying to kill you. Then it possessed the necromancer after he kidnapped you, and eventually used the necromancer's body to interrupt a murderer who was about to kill you."

I glanced at my sisters, then back to Ida. "So what are you trying to say?"

Ida's demeanor was so unlike that of a teenager that her image was almost jarring. "Adelaide, the dark magic came here tonight to protect you. It saw an angry warlock and got rid of him, and shut out the ghosts to keep us from interfering."

"So it didn't try to banish you?" I croaked.

She shook her head. "Bradley is with his brother now, unharmed."

I shuffled over to the couch and sat down. Even if the dark magic had tried to protect me tonight, I didn't think it was altruistic by any means. It had tried to possess me on multiple occasions. It might want me alive and well, but it still wanted to use me.

Yet that left one really big question. Why hadn't it just taken me tonight, when its power was at its highest?

Sleep tugged at me. My body and mind had both given all they had to give.

My sisters locked gazes, then looked back down to me.

"You go upstairs and get some rest," Luna said. "We'll finish the wards."

"And we're calling mom," Callie added.

Logan moved toward the couch. "I'll track down Damon and call you in the morning." He looked toward my sisters. "Your mom will be able to protect her?"

They both nodded, their expressions solemn.

I snuggled Spooky and didn't have the strength to argue. I hadn't wanted to involve my mom and cousin Amber because they would come in and take over my life. Now I'd be glad for the break. Plus, anything was better than the alternative, when the alternative was dark magic obsessing over me like a jealous ex.

CHAPTER FOURTEEN

I rolled over in bed, groaning as a line of sunshine cutting through the window hit my eyes. My head throbbed from all of the adrenaline of the previous evening. Or maybe I just needed to drink some water.

I sat up and rubbed my eyes, then looked around for Spooky. He was usually with me when I woke up, but he was nowhere to be seen.

I started to get out of bed, then froze at the sound of voices downstairs. I recognized cousin Amber first, then a lower murmur that had to be my mom. I supposed I shouldn't be surprised that they would come over first thing in the morning.

With a heavy sigh, I grabbed my phone from my nightstand and looked at the time.

What! I blinked, then looked at the phone again.

There was no way it could be ten o'clock. I already was going to be pushing it with finishing all the baking, now I'd gone and slept half of the morning away. I could have sworn I set an alarm.

Shaking my head in disgust, I got up and rushed through getting ready. Curls in a braid, torn jeans and a pale gray sweater I wouldn't mind getting flour on, a splash of water on my face, and a quick tooth brushing and I was ready to go.

With my phone in my back pocket I hurried out of my room and down the stairs, finding my mom, sisters, and cousin Amber in the kitchen. Spooky sat by his food dish, waiting for it to be filled.

He would have to wait a few minutes longer. I blinked at the counter, stunned by the array of baked goods lining every surface. They were just like I imagined, right down to the spooky donuts with black icing.

Unable to tear my eyes away from the pastries, I shuffled across the kitchen to give my mom a hug. "Did you do all of this?"

She pulled away from me, tucking a lock of hair the same ginger shade as mine behind an ear. "I just got here, sweetie."

I looked to Amber for a moment with her sleek black bob and charcoal pantsuit that probably cost a thousand bucks and quickly dismissed that notion, turning next to my sisters.

Callie still wore her basic top and jeans from the night before, her hair a frizzy mess. "Don't look at me."

And so I looked to Luna, who shook her head. "None of us did this, Addy. It was simply here when we woke up."

I walked toward the counter, stopping before the tray of donuts. I slowly reached my hand out like they might bite me, but my fingers settled around flaky dough without incident. I lifted it up to my face and observed it. It smelled wonderful. "So you're telling me someone broke into my house and did all of my baking for me?" Donut still in hand, I turned to look at everyone. "Was it Ida? Halloween is tomorrow, it's possible she could make this happen."

Amber crossed her arms and shook her head. "I sent her to watch after the warlock. It wasn't her."

I glanced at Luna. "I see you filled them in on everything."

My mom stepped toward me in a swirl of multi layered skirts. "We should have been filled in on everything sooner, Adelaide."

I stared her down. "I'm not a child, mom." I lifted the donut toward my face and took a bite.

"Adelaide!" my mom chided. "We don't know where those came from." She watched me helplessly as I chewed the bite I had taken, analyzing the quality.

The orange marmalade inside was perfect, just

sweet enough to balance out the less sweet dough. It wasn't imbued with magic, at least not my magic, since I didn't get any cozy feeling. And more importantly, it had no residue of dark magic. If the dark magic had done this, I would be able to sense it.

My mom glared at me as I took another bite.

"What?" I asked with my mouth half-full. "It's good."

Luna crossed her arms and rolled her eyes. "For all you knew those could have been poisoned."

I walked past her, still eating the donut as I opened a can of cat food for Spooky. "If someone wanted to poison me they could just slip it into my cup of coffee at the cafe. There would be no need to go to all this trouble."

"Unless they wanted to poison the whole town," she said to my back. "And they wanted to use you to do it."

That stopped me dead in my tracks. I looked down at the half eaten donut and regretted my decision, but nothing had happened yet, so it was probably fine.

I set the donut on the counter and filled Spooky's food dish, giving him a stroke as I set it down in front of him. "Maybe you saw something," I said to the cat. "Can you tell me who broke into my kitchen and baked everything?"

"She's not taking this seriously," Amber said

behind me.

"Oh I'm taking this very seriously," I said as I turned around. "Just like I'm taking two murders seriously. Fortunately now that all the baking is done, I can focus on that."

My mom sighed. "I'll admit, it was probably just friendly spirits helping you out. Strange things like this always occurred around Ida on Halloween."

"But why would they want to help me out?" I asked.

"You're a channeling witch. You have helped many spirits, and the spirit world is not without gratitude."

That was news to me, pleasant news for once. It was nice to be appreciated. "Well now that this is all ready I'm going to call Logan and see if he and Damon made any progress."

"But what about Halloween?" Amber asked. "There's no saying what might happen tonight."

I shrugged. "It's happening one way or another, there's nothing I can do about that. The dark magic can find me anywhere, and it broke through the wards on the house like they were nothing." I leaned against the counter. "All I can do is focus on the murders and hope they lead me to the necromancer. Once I catch that little rat I can make him tell me anything he knows about the dark magic."

Callie laughed. "I like this side of you, sis."

I might have made my sister happy, but cousin Amber didn't seem impressed. "Ida told us about the witch hunter."

I inhaled sharply. I really had just wanted to focus on the murder and not the possibility of my boyfriend being a witch hunter. "I don't think Max knows anything about our world, or what his father did to Ida."

Noticing the tears in my mom's eyes, I hesitated. My mom never cried.

She lifted her nose and steeled her expression. "None of us suspected what Isaac was."

She never talked about Ida's death, and now that I knew what had happened, I didn't want to make her start. I walked across the kitchen and gave her a hug. "I'll be careful, mom. I promise. But I'm not going to condemn him when he might not know anything. I have to find out for sure."

She met my eyes as I pulled away. "You always say you'll be careful, Adelaide, but you never are."

That one stung. I never meant to be reckless, but it did always seem to happen. "I really will be careful. I need to call Logan now. Other than any work on that front I'll stay home all day with you guys."

Amber stepped forward. "Oh, we're not staying home. Call your detective if you must, but Ida already told us that the living warlock is a scryer and clairvoyant. We are going to convince him to find the necromancer for us."

My jaw dropped. Here I'd been sure that everyone would want to stay far away from Damon. "And just how do you plan on convincing him?"

She put her hands on her hips. "Adelaide, Adelaide. We have a full coven. If that warlock has an ounce of survival instinct, he's going to help us."

Suddenly the few bites of donut I'd had felt like a lead weight in my stomach. I really didn't want to show up at Damon's door and threaten him, but I knew there was no swaying cousin Amber once she had set her mind to something, especially since my mom wasn't arguing.

I let out a heavy sigh. "Alright, but I'm making coffee first. Lots and lots of coffee." I moved toward the stove to boil water, but all of the baked goods were in the way. "And we need to box all of these up and get them to the cafe. If we're spending the day with a warlock, I won't have time to bake anything else."

"You really think they're safe to give to the general public?" Callie asked.

I handed her a pumpkin tart. "Eat up, we'll test everything first just to be sure."

I moved a tray aside to start the coffee, though my mind was already buzzing more than any amount of caffeine could cause.

CHAPTER FIFTEEN

I decided against calling Logan. If we were going to threaten Damon, I didn't want him around. And since we didn't know where Damon lived, we ended up at Divine Goddess Bookstore. My mom, Amber, and Spooky came with me while Callie and Luna delivered all of the baked goods to the Toasty Bean. We had tried everything, and none of us were dead yet, so it seemed like they were safe.

We could have summoned Ida to figure out where Damon lived—she had gone with Bradley to help him —but I wanted to learn whatever I could about him first. Meagan had at least met him before. Maybe she could tell me something useful. Something that would make him willingly work with us to find the necromancer.

I parked on the street and lifted Spooky as I got out of the car.

My mom and Amber both got out on the other side, the latter of whom looked over the hood toward the purple and silver sign. "How . . . tacky."

Clutching Spooky, I glanced at the sign, then shrugged. "I like it."

I led the way toward the door and the three of us went inside. It was busier than the previous day, mostly tourists looking for something ghoulishly festive to do before the parties took place in the evening. A few of them noticed Spooky and looked me up and down, but quickly went back to what they were doing. Even with the cat, I probably looked less like a witch than anyone else in the shop. If only they knew the truth.

I wove my way to the front of the store, finding Meagan behind the register. She wore a sleek black dress with a massive black witch's hat atop her blonde curls. Her eyes went a little wide as she noticed me, then she glanced at my mom and Amber just behind me. She quickly finished bagging up her customer's purchases, then leaned her hands on the counter as we stepped up for our turn.

"Can I help you, detective?"

Amber snorted behind me.

Ignoring her, I smiled pleasantly and stepped closer to the counter. It was a bad idea to impersonate a homicide detective, but she had drawn that conclusion on her own. I might as well work with it. "I just have a few more questions for you. Do you have a moment?"

Frowning, she looked past me to her busy shop. "Not really. Is it urgent?"

Tired of holding him, I set Spooky on the counter. I wasn't about to leave empty-handed. "I'm just wondering how well you know Damon Maxwell."

Her lips parted, and she stared at me for just a second. Apparently I had caught her off guard. "He's Bradley's brother. What about him? Is he a suspect?"

"Not a suspect," I assured before she got any funny ideas. "Do you know him well?"

She started to shake her head, then stopped. "I don't really know him, but he did throw the party where we met that creepy guy we told you about."

Her reaction to the mention of Damon had me hesitating to ask for his address. If she thought he was a suspect, she might just go over there and question him herself, and she would have no idea what she was getting herself into.

"Do you attend many parties?" I asked instead. I knew I was grasping at straws, but if I could get in on these parties maybe I could find the necromancer even if Damon wouldn't agree to help us.

She shrugged. "A few. Our circle of friends usually take turns throwing them. The next one is a costume party tonight for Halloween, but after Alison—" her lip trembled, then she shook her head. "I'm not going, but I can give you the details if it's important."

I resisted the urge to give Amber a smug smile. Her and my mom had stayed quiet, not blowing my cover, and I didn't want to risk an outburst. "That would be very helpful, thank you. Are Nina and Jodi going?"

She shook her head. "The three of us are going to spend Halloween together in honor of Alison." She took a sticky note and wrote down an address, then handed it to me.

"That's a nice sentiment." I smiled and took the note. "Thanks for the information."

I lifted Spooky and turned to leave, then nearly stumbled as a word echoed through my mind.

Witch.

I quickly righted myself and kept walking, looking down at the cat in my arms. "Did you say something?" I whispered.

Receiving only silence in reply, I hurried out to the street with my mom and Amber following close behind me. I moved away from the door, then glanced back through the bookshop window, barely able to spot Meagan past her customers and the tall shelves of books.

My mom stood close and put a hand on my shoulder. "Is something wrong?"

I watched Meagan a moment longer, then shook my head. "I could swear that Spooky just told me Meagan is a witch, but that can't be right."

Amber scoffed, "She's definitely not a witch. I can always tell."

My mom rolled her eyes. "We can *all* always tell. That's part of being what we are. That girl doesn't have an ounce of real magic to her."

Despite my mom's words, I still felt uneasy. I looked down at the address in my free hand. "Let's summon Ida and find Damon. I want to ask him about these parties."

"Do you think it's important?" my mom asked as we started walking.

"Bradley and Alison both went to one of these parties a week ago. Now they're both dead. It's at least a place to start."

"Parties with warlocks." Amber shivered on my other side. "Who would want to go to one of those?"

I shook my head as we reached my car. Who would want to go to parties with warlocks? Why witches, necromancers, and maybe even a murderer.

Maybe Callie would get to use her costume after all.

CHAPTER SIXTEEN

Logan called me as we pulled up to the address Ida had provided. She was waiting by the front door, looking nervous. The place was practically a mansion. I found myself wondering what Damon Maxwell did for a living. I stepped out of the car with my cat, my mom, and Amber. I supposed we were about to find out, if he would even talk to us.

"Where are you?" Logan's voice came through the phone as I shut my car door with my hip.

I glanced toward the house, wishing I hadn't answered. If I lied to Logan now, and things went wrong with Damon . . . "I'm at Damon Maxwell's house. I want to ask him about that party the girls mentioned. Apparently there's going to be another one tonight."

A moment of silence, then, "Addy, why are you questioning suspects without me?"

Holding Spooky across one shoulder, I leaned my butt against the car. "Is he a suspect?"

"Well he won't work with me to find his brother's body, which makes me think he wants to find it first. Or maybe he already has it and wants to dispose of it."

I thought of Damon's anger the previous night, then his confusion and hurt at seeing Bradley's ghost. "I really don't think he killed his brother."

"Regardless, you shouldn't be questioning anyone without me. How did you find out about this party anyhow?"

Spooky started struggling against my arm, so I let him down to the ground. "Meagan told me about it. I figured if we can't find anything out through Damon, we'll go to the party. Between me, my mom, and my sisters, if there's anything with enough magic to sneak up and kill a warlock in broad daylight, we'll find it."

He sighed loudly. "Wait there. If you're going to question Damon, I'm going to be there too."

"He might speak more freely without you here," I countered. *And cousin Amber won't be able to threaten him with a cop around*, I added in my head.

My mom and Amber walked around the car as the front door to the mansion opened, and Damon stepped outside.

"I've got to go, Logan," I said into my phone. "I promise I'll be careful." I hung up, then glanced around my feet, but Spooky had scampered off somewhere.

Damon Maxwell marched toward us like an angry storm. The gash on his forehead and light bruising on his jaw were painfully apparent. He wore cream slacks with a white button up, no suit jacket. The first few buttons of his shirt were undone, and his hair was mussed, like he had been working all night.

And I knew he had. According to Ida, he had been scrying for Bradley's body, but he had been unable to locate it. Bradley appeared in the doorway beside Ida, and both ghosts floated after Damon.

Damon's angry eyes scanned my mom and Amber as he reached us, then settled on me. "What are you doing here? It's bad enough you sent your dead aunt to spy on me."

I noted Ida's furious expression as she floated closer. Looking worried, Bradley grabbed her arm and held her back.

Damon didn't notice either of them. His attention was all on me. "Well? Are you going to tell me what you're doing here, or are you just going to stare at me like an idiot?"

I crossed my arms and jutted out my hip. "I'll tell you once you stop acting so hostile and we can have a civil conversation. Let's not forget, you're the one that attacked me in my home. If anyone should be angry here, it's me."

He glared at me. "I don't want your help, and I don't need it. I'm going to find my brother's killer and make them pay."

I lifted a brow. "What makes you think you'll fare any better against something that could sneak up on a warlock in broad daylight?"

He glanced back at his brother's ghost.

Bradley frowned and shook his head.

I really wished I could see Damon's expression as he continued to watch his brother.

Bradley floated a little closer, making a shooing gesture with his hands.

I suspected accepting my help had already been a lengthy conversation between them. Bradley didn't want his brother to end up down a river too.

His spine painfully stiff, Damon turned back toward me. "Fine." He glanced around his driveway. The path leading up to the house was a long one, surrounded by several acres of trees and grass. "Come inside," he decided. "The house is warded. You never know who might be watching."

I glanced at my mom and Amber, who both shrugged. Bradley and Alison might not have had any enemies, but I had a feeling maybe Damon did. Of course, I couldn't throw stones. I had dark magic and a necromancer after me. Maybe once Damon chilled out a bit we could compare enemies.

He gave my little car a look of distaste, then turned and led the way back toward the house.

I scowled at his back and followed, biting my tongue. He was giving me what I wanted, after all. Now wasn't the time to get indignant about him judging the quality of my car.

My mom and Amber fell into step beside me, and the ghosts took up the rear. I still didn't see Spooky anywhere, but if he was snooping in Damon's house, I didn't want to draw any extra attention by looking for him.

We reached the house and I started to follow Damon through the front door, but hesitated when I felt his wards. I took another slow step, and it was like electricity coursing through my veins.

Damon stopped on the dark slate tiles of the entryway and turned back to me.

I just barely managed a glare. Nothing looked out of place in the wide room—from the gleaming furniture to the modern light fixtures—but an invisible electric wall held me in place.

With a smug smile, Damon waved his hand and the feeling of electricity vanished. "I just wanted to test that they were still working. The wards on your house were so weak I got worried."

"And yet, the dark magic tossed you out so easily," I snarled.

Though I got a laugh out of Amber behind me, I realized I'd misspoke.

Damon marched back toward me. "If I find out you're working with that dark magic, or if it had anything to do with my brother's death—"

My mom stepped up beside me and held out a hand. "I will not stand here and listen to you accuse my daughter of working with that . . . thing. She is here to help you and your brother, and you will treat her with respect."

Damon's eyes widened. He looked like he had about ten different scathing replies on the tip of his tongue, but finally shut his jaw with a click. "This way," he snapped, then turned and strode further into the house.

Bradley floated through the wall next to the door. "Sorry about him. He's just stressed out."

Amber tsked at him. "We expect no pleasantries from warlocks." She followed in the direction Damon had gone, her spine perfectly straight beneath her charcoal suit jacket.

Bradley floated after her, leaving me momentarily alone with my mom and Ida.

"Be on your guard," my mom said to both of us. "He may not have killed his brother, but he still can't be trusted." With that, she followed in the direction the others had gone.

Ida floated near my shoulder. "Where's Spooky?" she whispered.

I shook my head. "Spying, I hope."

"I'll find him," she assured, and then she was gone.

I took one last look around the grand foyer in all of its dark, imposing glory, then stepped into the den of the wolf.

Not that I was intimidated or anything like that. I'd dealt with plenty of wolves in my time.

CHAPTER SEVENTEEN

I followed the sound of voices down the long hallway, past a gleaming kitchen and several closed doors. I was wondering more and more what Damon did for work. He was the polar opposite of Bradley, or so it seemed.

I found my mom and the others in Damon's office, gathered around a map spread out on an oak desk that probably cost more than my car. A crystal pendulum hung from the ceiling, centered over the map.

"It's not like we can steal your magic," Amber was saying. "Just show us what happens when you try to scry for Bradley."

"They're just trying to help," the ghost in question added, floating near his brother's shoulder.

Damon raised his eyes to me as I stepped into the room.

I ran a hand across the expensive bookcase lining the nearby wall. "What do you do for work, anyway?" I ran my fingers across runes etched into the edges of the bookcase. My heart skipped a beat as I realized why they looked familiar. They were from the Celtic Ogham.

"That's none of your concern," Damon snapped. "Now either offer help as promised, or get out."

My mom gave him a warning look. Though she was tall, she was thin like Callie and not overly imposing, but that look could freeze the most hardened criminal in his tracks.

Damon stared at her for a heartbeat, sucked his teeth, then sighed. "My apologies," he forced the words through his clenched jaw. "But I'm sure you can all understand my reservations."

I approached the desk and looked down at the map, still feeling shaken by the runes. "We can understand your reservations, but if you're quite through maybe you can show us what happens when you scry for Bradley's body. In return we can share our theories about his killer." *Unless you're the killer,* I thought. *Alison's killer.* The runes were too big of a coincidence.

He leaned forward, spreading his hands across the map. "Fine."

He bowed his head, and within seconds I felt the

first trickle of magic. I'd known from his wards that he was strong, but I hadn't expected this. I recalled a memory from childhood, running home in the rain. Lightning had struck right across the street from me. I had felt the electric charge and knew just how close to death or serious injury I had come. It was a feeling I would never forget, and standing this close to Damon, I was experiencing it all over again.

My mom stepped back as the pendulum began to swing. Amber stepped closer, which let you know just the type of woman she was. Stepping closer to danger and power rather than away from it. Bradley floated near his brother's shoulder, used to the show.

I felt barely able to draw breath as the pendulum started circling the map, moving of its own accord. Suddenly the smooth arcs of its movement became erratic. It shot back and forth, pointing everywhere—or nowhere—when it should have been settling on a single point.

With a heavy breath, Damon stepped back.

The pendulum swung back to the center of the map, then stilled.

"When Bradley first went missing," Damon explained, "the pendulum went to two specific locations, one of them your house." He raised his eyes from the map to land on my face. "After I came back home from confronting you, it started doing this. I think someone is interfering with my scrying."

Damon's electric magic was still a tickling memory on my skin. I lifted my hands to rub the goosebumps on my arms beneath my sweater. "Do you know anyone with that much power?"

He let out a husky laugh, and suddenly I was aware of the sheen of sweat on his brow. Fighting with the interfering force had cost him. "A coven of witches could do it, but with three of you here that theory has been proven incorrect."

My mom stepped closer to the desk. "You were testing us."

Damon straightened his back. Though his hands remained limp at his sides, the threat was there. "Can you blame me?" His eyes darted to the open doorway before my mom could answer. "Someone is here."

I winced. "That's probably Lo—err, Detective White. He called me just as I was pulling up."

Damon marched around the desk and strode past me out of the office and down the hall.

I hurried after him, leaving my mom and Amber with Bradley. By the time I caught up he was already at the door, opening it with an irritated jerk.

Logan stood outside looking considerably less rumpled than the last time I saw him.

Damon stood blocking the doorway. "I told you I would call if I found anything."

I had to give Logan points for not backing down from the anger in Damon's voice. He gave Damon a bored expression and looked past his shoulder to where I was peeking over it. "Ms. O'Shea, may I speak with you for a moment?"

I tapped Damon's shoulder for him to move aside.

After a second of hesitation, he stepped to his right and looked down at me. "Make it quick, you still need to uphold your part of the bargain."

I fought to hide my discomfort. He was going to be *pissed* when he learned that the only information I had to share about Bradley's killer was my suspicion about the necromancer and the parties.

Damon silently waited for me to step outside, then shut the door behind me.

Logan crossed his arms, bunching up his suit jacket. "What did you do to make him so angry?"

I wrinkled my nose. "I think he's just as angry with you as he is with me. He was *not* pleased when I said it was probably you at the door."

Logan started walking away from the house, and I followed. "He doesn't trust me because I'm working with you. He thinks you'll cloud my judgment."

We stopped walking as we neared Logan's car parked next to mine, then I turned toward him.

"Damon had runes from the Celtic Ogham etched into his bookcase."

I didn't get the surprise I'd expected. "I saw them last night before he kicked me out. I asked about them, and he said that his family has always kept to Celtic traditions. He didn't seem to know why I was asking about them."

"So Allison was just a coincidence?" I asked.

"Maybe, maybe not. He didn't try to keep me from seeing them though, and he let you see them now. Although I'm surprised he let you in."

"He thought my family was messing with his scrying," I explained. "He let us in to test us, so now he knows that's not the case."

Logan leaned against the hood of his car and lifted a brow. "And do you know who is?"

I shook my head. "The necromancer was powerful, but so is Damon. If the two of them were in a fight, I would put my money on the warlock."

"And what's the difference between a warlock and a necromancer?"

I leaned against the hood of his car beside him, glad to have a little break from Damon's ire. "Warlocks are basically just like male witches. While our powers vary, they are an extension of our will. They come from within, and from our innate connection to the earth. Necromancers are different. They draw their magic from the spirit world. Their power is stolen."

"And the necromancer wanted to use you to steal more of that power."

I lifted a hand to shield my eyes from the sun as I looked at him. "You catch on quick."

"Would the necromancer target Damon and Bradley for the same reason?"

I shrugged. "Maybe. I'm sure he at least knows about them. If Damon didn't kill Allison, I believe the necromancer did, but he probably didn't kill Bradley."

"Why just Alison?"

I looked back toward the house. I didn't see anyone in any of the windows, but I had an uncomfortable feeling like I was being watched. "Alison's ghost hasn't shown up. Maybe she just moved on, but she was murdered. She had a reason to stick around and find me. The necromancer could have easily prevented her from doing so."

Logan nodded along. "And Bradley's ghost did find you. So we have two murderers."

"And one is something far from human," I added. "I felt Damon's magic today. If Bradley had even half of his power, he would have been difficult to take out."

"Wonderful," Logan sighed. "At least without a body, I won't have to worry about covering it up."

He'd said it like a joke, but I agreed with him.

Whatever had killed Bradley was probably something that couldn't be arrested. We'd have to take care of it ourselves.

We both looked up as Ida appeared near the driveway, then floated toward us. Spooky trotted behind her.

She reached us, then glanced toward the house before whispering, "Thank goddess you're out here. There's something you both need to see." She disappeared from sight, but her voice lingered. "Follow Spooky. I'll make sure you don't get caught."

I stood and turned to Logan. "Ida found something. We need to follow Spooky."

Logan glanced down at the cat then stood as Spooky darted away from the driveway. We hurried after him, and I could only hope Damon wasn't watching us from any of the windows. I didn't think my mom would let him out of her sight though, so we should be safe, but he'd be wondering why I hadn't come back soon.

Spooky trotted across the grass and behind a tree.

I ran after him, pulling ahead of Logan as my mind swam with questions. We ran until we reached the fence bordering Damon's property, and there Spooky waited.

I looked down at what he had found, then held a

hand to my heart. The nausea came next, and I staggered away as Logan reached us.

He made the connection just as quickly as I had, though he didn't seem anywhere near as shocked. "That looks just like one of the hiking boots Bradley was wearing the day he died."

I swallowed the lump in my throat and looked down at the lone boot. It must have been removed before Bradley's body took a trip down the river. Not only was it not damp, it was covered in blood.

CHAPTER EIGHTEEN

L ogan and I both stood staring at the bloody shoe. It was definitely Bradley's. Question was, what was it doing on his brother's property?

Spooky waited patiently near the shoe, watching us both.

"Should we call someone?" I asked Logan.

His brow furrowed. "If we call this in, it may be enough to launch an investigation. But if some supernatural force killed Bradley . . . "

"You might end up needing to cover for me again," I finished for him.

Sunlight cut across his dark features as he met my eyes. "I don't like this, Addy. I don't like not calling in a murder."

I took a shaky breath. "So call it in. Get a search

warrant for Damon's house. I will try to stay out of it and work on things from my end, but either way, I need to get back in there before Damon realizes something is wrong."

He stepped around the shoe to grab my arm. "You are *not* going back in there."

I was shaking and scared, yet I still somehow managed to summon some indignance. "I most certainly am."

Still holding my arm, he stepped closer to me and lowered his voice. "Addy, Damon might have murdered his brother. I can't let you go back in the house."

I pointedly stepped back and pulled my arm out of his grasp. "My mom and Amber are still in that house, and I think it's more likely that someone planted this shoe here. You were gone when Damon came looking for me. He really thought I had killed his brother. I may not like him, but I don't think he did this. And now with the runes? It seems like someone is framing him for both murders."

"It could all be an act."

Spooky walked toward my feet and twined around my ankles, signaling that he was ready to go. "Maybe it is an act, and if so, I want him convinced that I believe it." I bent down and picked up my cat.

Logan watched me. I felt bad arguing—I knew he was just worried about me—but I couldn't back down.

He sighed. "I'll go in with you, and I'll call in the shoe after we leave."

I shook my head. "You know as well as I do that we need to work on this separately now. If anything happens that you shouldn't know about . . . I don't want you covering for me again." I started to walk away, but hesitated. "I'll let you know if I come across any more pieces of Bradley."

He watched me as I walked away, but didn't try to stop me again. Part of me wished he had never come. If Spooky had led me to the shoe on my own, I wouldn't have reported it. Things were getting weird, and the human police didn't need to be involved.

As I neared my car in the driveway, I wondered at what point I had decided to become a supernatural crime fighter. I was a baker, not a detective. I didn't belong in the world of murder mysteries.

Yet here I was, wondering if Damon had actually killed his brother, and what I was going to do about it. I held Spooky close, then walked back toward the house, opened the door, and went through it. It was the bravest thing I'd done all day.

I shut the door behind me then leaned against it as the sound of voices headed my way. Everyone came into the foyer, preparing to leave. Ida's relief was clear when she saw me.

"If we're done with the questions," Damon snapped at her. "I have work to do."

"We're done," my mom said, walking toward me. "We'll let you know if we locate the necromancer, and we expect you to do the same."

It seemed my mom and Amber had filled him in on our suspicions about the necromancer, but I sure hoped they didn't tell him about the party. After discovering Bradley's shoe, I definitely didn't want Damon to know I was going.

Damon finally turned his attention to me. "Was that cat with you the whole time?"

"I had the windows open for him in the car. Scout's honor." I held up a hand with the middle three fingers up.

He narrowed his eyes for a moment, then seemed to dismiss it. "Come, Bradley. We'll begin our search for this necromancer."

Bradley put a spectral hand on his brother's shoulder. "I need to go with Addy. She'll keep me from fading and forgetting anything that might be important."

Damon stared at Bradley like he had just grown a second head. Then he gnawed his lip, and I realized he was holding back tears.

"I'll take care of him," I promised, feeling more confused than ever. Either Damon was innocent, or he was one hell of an actor.

He gave me a sharp nod. "See that you do." He batted a tear from his eye, then turned and walked further into the house, leaving us to let ourselves out.

Bradley watched his brother go, then turned to me. "I should make sure he's all right."

I nodded. "Meet us at the house whenever you want." *Which hopefully wouldn't be soon*, I added in my head. I wanted time to discuss things with my family in private first.

As Bradley floated away, I looked to my mom and Amber. "We'll talk in the car."

I opened the door and turned to leave, noticing that Logan's car was now gone. Either he had decided not to call in the shoe, or he was going to leave another anonymous tip. I wouldn't call and ask him. He wanted the murders solved, but he wanted them solved in a way that could be explained to the police, and at this point, I simply couldn't guarantee it.

Ida led the way out through the open door, then fell back to float at my side as we walked toward my car. "I stalled as long as I could," she whispered. "Did you see it?"

I nodded, my expression grim, then opened the

Once we managed to park, we all got out of the car. I carried Spooky as we walked past tourists standing in the street toward the cafe. Everyone had pastries in hand, even though I had planned for most of them to not sell until evening.

Amber stopped in front of the cafe and peered through the window. "Oh boy, I think I'll wait out here. I don't relish the thought of pushing through that crowd."

I moved to her side to see what she was talking about, and could hardly believe my eyes. I'd had crowds in the cafe before, but it was standing room only. Most of the patrons were in costume, so it looked like some weird monster party inside.

My mom stepped close to Amber as two customers dressed as wizards left the cafe, pressing her back against the window to let them pass. "We'll see you when you get out."

I handed Spooky to my mom, then went inside. I needed to make sure Evie wasn't selling all of the pastries before the busiest part of the festival had even officially begun.

Inside, I wove my way through the crowd, catching a few dirty looks from people who didn't realize I was the owner. Richie and Evie were both behind the counter, which I finally reached with a few people cursing behind my back.

"What's going on?" I asked Evie. "I'm seeing tons of people with the pastries. Will there be any left for tonight?"

She swiped a hand across her forehead, smoothing it back against her tight curls pulled into twin braids. "Well you baked enough to feed an army." She gestured past Richie to the stacked trays on the back counter.

My eyes widened. "My sisters brought all of those this morning?" There were four times as many trays as what had been in my kitchen.

Evie raised her brows. "No, your sisters just delivered the final batch. The rest were here when I opened up."

I shut my gaping jaw. "Oh, of course. Sorry, I'm just frazzled today."

"I imagine with all of that baking. Why don't you go home and rest? Richie and I have things covered." Evie turned her attention to the impatient customer behind me. "What can I get for you?"

Richie finished with the coffee he was making and extended it around me to another waiting customer, then gave me a little salute and went to make the next order.

I stepped away from the counter to get out of the way, but my gaze lingered on all the pastries. We had only tested the ones in my house. What if the rest weren't safe?

I glanced around at all the customers, happily drinking their coffees and eating their sweets. Evie had been selling the pastries all day, and everyone seemed fine. I pushed away the air of foreboding closing in around me and made my way to the door, finding my mom and Amber still waiting outside with Spooky.

I ushered them further from the door, then whispered, "More pastries showed up here this morning."

Amber stared at me for a moment. "Are you serious? And you've had no visits from spirits to claim credit?"

I shook my head.

My mom lifted Spooky so that his front legs were resting across her shoulder. "I wonder why only one batch was delivered to the house."

Amber took in my worried expression. "Don't fret, dear. We tested everything." Despite her words, her voice shook. "I'm sure it was just friendly spirits, even if they don't want to claim the credit."

I clutched my stomach, feeling ill with nerves. "I sure hope so."

"Everyone seems fine," Amber assured more steadily. "Now let's go meet your sisters. We have a lot of planning to do before the party tonight."

I let out a long breath and pushed my worries

about the pastries away. It was too late to do anything about it now. I pulled my phone out of my pocket to check the time, then all of my worries came flooding back. I had a missed call and two texts from Max. I checked my notification settings and realized I had put my phone on silent after the call from Logan.

I lifted my eyes to find Amber staring at me intently. "It's the witch hunter, isn't it?"

I glanced around at the crowd, but nobody had looked our way. "Keep it down," I hissed. "And he's not a witch hunter."

I led the way back toward my car, letting my mom carry Spooky. I barely noticed the passersby as we went. I needed to call Max back, or at least send him a text to let him know everything was okay, but what was I going to tell him? I had a feeling faking another migraine wasn't going to cut it. If he was a witch hunter, staying away was smart, but if he wasn't? All of this dancing around was going to ruin our relationship before it even had a chance to start.

It left me with only one option. I had to find out what he knew, and to do that, I needed to see him.

Tonight.

CHAPTER TWENTY

We arrived at my house before Callie and Luna. That they were taking this long to pick out costumes for everyone had me a little nervous, but maybe things were just mostly sold out. I walked into the house with Spooky and set him down, debating how I would tell my mom and Amber that I was going to call Max.

My decision was quickly made for me. When Amber went to the bathroom, my mom put a hand on my shoulder. "I think you should call him and invite him over. You'll feel better once you know for sure, and we don't need you distracted tonight."

I managed a weak smile. "Thanks mom, but how am I supposed to tell if he's actually a witch hunter?"

Her mischievous grin had me a little unnerved. "Just invite him over, and leave that part to me. Tell him you need help baking a few last things for the cafe."

"But the cafe is completely stocked," I countered.

She rolled her eyes. "Just do it, Adelaide. I'm going to make some coffee. It will be easier to convince Amber to help me if she's caffeinated."

I watched her go into the kitchen, then pulled out my phone. Nervous, I reread Max's two texts. The first asked if I needed any ingredients, and the second asked if I was alright. If he wasn't a witch hunter I was going to feel like a jerk for making him jump through so many hoops.

I hit his name and pushed the call button, then lifted the phone to my ear.

He answered on the first ring. Had he been waiting for my call? Guilt and apprehension made my knees weak.

"Hey, sorry I missed your call," I said as I staggered toward the sofa then slumped down onto the cushions.

"Don't worry about it," he replied. "Sorry to bother you if you were busy."

I took a steadying breath. "I just went to check on the cafe. It was totally packed, so now I'm back home ready to bake, but I forgot a few ingredients."

"Say no more. What do you need?"

He was just too darn nice. But was it all an act? I rattled off a list of ingredients. I already had pretty much everything I needed, so I might have to hide a few things before he showed up. "And Max?" I added.

"Yes?"

"I know you're terrible at baking, but do you want to keep me company? I mean my family is here too," I quickly amended, "but I like your company better."

He laughed. "Give me some time to pick everything up, then I'll head over."

I smiled against my phone. He simply couldn't be a witch hunter. "See you soon."

I hung up and lowered my phone as my mom walked back in from the kitchen with two cups of coffee in hand. "Is it done?"

Amber came down the stairs. "Is what done?"

My mom walked across the room and handed her a cup of coffee.

Amber raised an eyebrow as she took it. "You're about to say something I won't like, aren't you?"

"Adelaide invited Max over so we can figure out once and for all if he's a witch hunter."

Amber scowled. "Don't we have enough on our plates as it is?"

My mom smiled sweetly. "We do, but Adelaide is trying to solve two murders. One a warlock, and one a mundane who identified as a witch. Who do you think would want to kill them?"

My jaw dropped. And here I had thought my mom

was on my side. "You don't seriously think Max killed them," I balked.

She turned toward me and took a sip of her coffee, then lowered her mug. "His father led my sister to her death. I won't let the same happen to you. If he's innocent, then we'll back off, but it's in all of our best interests to find out."

I really didn't like the scary look in my mom's eyes. "Just what are you going to do to find out?"

"We are going to haunt him and gauge his reaction."

I took a step toward her. "But what if he doesn't know anything?" I demanded. "You're going to scare a mundane out of his wits and he's going to go running far away from me."

"It's almost Halloween," Amber said, stepping closer to my mom. "If he's innocent, we'll just say it was all a prank."

I shook my head in disbelief as they both stood there and sipped their coffees.

"You're both completely insane."

I turned as the door opened behind me, and Callie and Luna came inside.

Callie grinned, holding up one of the costumes draped across her arm.

I stared at the costume in stunned silence.

It was official. I was completely surrounded by

lunatics.

I WENT to my room to freshen up before Max arrived, leaving the offending costume on my bed. When I returned from the bathroom, Spooky sat next to it, sniffing the black fabric.

I put my hands on my hips and looked down, wondering how I was going to get out of wearing the ridiculous get up. "Callie thinks she's real funny," I muttered to Spooky.

Of course she'd want to dress me up just like my familiar.

I reached down and lifted up the sleeve of the skin-tight black catsuit, rubbing the thin fabric between my fingers. There was a matching black wig to cover my ginger curls, and a mask that would cover the upper half of my face. The mask looked like black lace, but was actually lightweight painted metal with two cat ears poking up from the top. I didn't mind the mask or the wig, but the catsuit would leave little to the imagination. I was more of a chunky sweater and jeans kind of girl.

I went to my window as I heard a car pull up outside, spotting Max parking on the street below. I watched him get out. He raked a hand through his light brown hair and tugged at the hem of his dark green fleece, unaware of me watching him. He opened the back seat, and pulled out two grocery bags.

I glanced back at Spooky as Max headed toward the front door. "I hope you'll make sure my mom doesn't get carried away. And if Bradley appears, keep him in line too." In truth, I was a little worried Bradley hadn't shown up yet. I hoped everything was okay.

Spooky stared back at me for a moment, then hopped off the bed and trotted toward the bedroom door.

I walked across the room and opened it for him, then followed him out before heading down the stairs to answer the door, but my mom reached it first.

I peered over her shoulder as she greeted Max, taking one of the full shopping bags from his arm. "It's so nice of you to come help Addy. The rest of us would probably do more harm than good."

She stepped back for him to come inside, and I took her place, taking the other bag. "Don't listen to her. They're just too lazy to help me," I joked.

Max grinned, shutting the door behind him. "Well I'm happy to step in either way." He approached and gave me a kiss on the cheek.

"Well I'll just leave you two to it," my mom said, setting down the grocery bag before heading for the stairs.

"Let's go into the kitchen," I said, clutching the second bag against my chest.

"Addy, wait." Max put a hand on my arm before I could walk away. "I feel like there's something you really need to tell me."

I scanned his concerned face. If I just admitted that I was a witch . . . I opened my mouth, but the words froze on my tongue. I realized part of me felt like maybe he actually was a witch hunter, and I didn't want to face the truth. I'd been enjoying dating him, and it had been a *really* long time since I actually enjoyed dating someone. I didn't want it to end.

"Addy?" he questioned, his voice quiet.

He started to let his hand drop, but I quickly stepped toward him. "Max, I'm a—"

The lights flickered, then went out.

Max tore his gaze from my face to look around. "Did the power just go out?"

The stairs creaked, though no one walked down them. Max's gaze followed the sound.

I swallowed the lump in my throat. Scaring a confession out of him was stupid. I was the one who was scared, and *I* was the one who should be making a confession.

"Max," I started again, then a chill wind swept through the room, followed by the feel of my mom's magic.

Max held out a hand, testing the wind now ruffling his hair. He stepped closer to me. "Addy, what's going on?"

I finally set down the grocery bag, then took his hand. He was totally confused. He really didn't know anything about my world. Ida was wrong.

The wind picked up more, accompanied by howling. I knew most of it was coming from my mom. Illusions were a strength of hers.

Max pulled me close. I could feel his heart beating against my cheek. "Addy." His voice came out raspy with fear.

This wasn't the right way to go about things. I pulled away from him and shouted, "Stop!"

The wind died down as if it had never existed.

Max looked to me, his eyes wide.

I should have been honest from the start. "Max, I'm a witch. And before you go disbelieving me, I can prove it."

He stared at me. I prepared myself for laughter, or outright denial. He took a step toward me, then grabbed my hand. "Addy, I know."

CHAPTER TWENTY-ONE

I tugged my hand from Max's grip as footsteps came thundering down the stairs.

My mom reached the living room first, her hair flying wildly around her face on currents of her own power. "Step away from my daughter!"

Max held up his hands, palms outward. "Now hold on a minute—"

Amber, my sisters, and Ida crowded around my mom. Luna lifted her hands. "Should I hex him?" she asked.

Max backed away until he hit the closed door. With his eyes locked on my family, he asked, "Addy, what's going on?"

I looked between him and my family, knowing we were walking a fine edge. My mom, Amber, and Luna could all do some serious damage with their offensive magic. Callie wasn't as dangerous, but she sure wouldn't be stopping them.

I held up a hand to keep them at bay, then turned my attention to Max. "You already knew that I'm a witch?"

He winced, but nodded. "I'm sorry, I didn't want to push you to tell me until you were ready."

"Your father was a witch hunter," my mom growled. "He killed my sister. You expect us to believe you are not of the same ilk?"

"What? No!" Max started to step forward, then froze as my mom lifted her hands.

My heart was pounding so hard, I felt like I might faint. "Max, how did you know I was a witch? Who told you?"

His brows knit together. "Addy, no one had to tell me. I can just . . . sense things. It's why I'm so good with animals."

As if on cue, Spooky strutted into the room from the kitchen. He sat down near Max's feet and looked up at me. *Honestly, you think I would sit on the lap of a witch hunter?*

I blinked at my familiar, stunned that I had actually heard him.

You're getting better at listening.

"Adelaide," my mom said as I stared at my cat. "I think you should come over here with us."

I ignored her and looked up to Max. "We know your dad was a witch hunter. He caused my aunt's death."

His utter shock seemed genuine. "She was your aunt?"

Ida gasped. "He knew about my death! Addy, get away from him!"

I ignored her. "Max, I think it's time for you to tell me everything you know."

He glanced at my family, then back to me. "Maybe we could have some privacy?"

"And let you harm her?" my mom interrupted. "I think not."

I gave Max an apologetic smile. "Sorry, but I think the time for secrets between any of us has passed."

His shoulders slumped as he nervously raked a hand through his hair. "I guess that's fair. I suppose I should start with my father. Or actually, with my father's father. He was the real witch hunter, and he's the one that made my dad hurt that girl—your aunt. My dad spent his entire life regretting what he did. When he realized I could . . . sense things, he told me about our family history. He wanted me to be prepared. He didn't want me to end up like him."

"What do you mean, you can sense things?" I asked.

He blushed. It took him a few seconds to find the

words, "Emotions. Sometimes I can sense emotions, or other things. I think I can sense your magic too. I wasn't sure if you were a witch, but after everything my dad had told me, I thought it likely."

I glanced at my family, all listening quietly. My sisters seem convinced, but my mom and Amber both aimed harsh glares at Max. I couldn't read Ida's expression. Had it made a difference for her to hear that Max's father regretted what he had done?

I turned back to Max. "If you could sense what I was, why not tell me sooner?"

He took a long breath, then let it out. "I don't know. I didn't know how to go about it. At first I thought maybe you didn't even realize what you were, but then with the glowing animals, I knew that you knew. I decided I should wait for you to tell me when you were ready. You seemed really intent on hiding it."

I let out a sigh of my own. All of the hiding and lies, all for nothing. "That's why you let things go so easily with the glowing animals. You never pushed me on it."

He nodded.

I looked back toward my family. I knew he could be lying to me, and I might be in danger, but he had known the entire time what I was, and he had never tried to hurt me. "I believe him," I said.

"So do we," Callie and Luna said in unison.

My mom and Amber locked gazes, then my mom stepped forward. She kept walking until she was face to face with Max. She looked up at him. "If you hurt my daughter—"

"I would *never* hurt your daughter." Max stared back at her.

I moved toward them both. "Mom, please. I can take care of myself. Spooky doesn't think he's a witch hunter either."

She whipped her gaze toward me, her chocolate brown eyes wide and mouth slightly agape. "He spoke to you?"

"Yep, he told me he would never sit in the lap of a witch hunter."

"Wait," Max interrupted. "You can talk to your cat?"

Now it was my turn to blush. I shrugged. "Welcome to my world, I guess."

"Cross your fingers that you survive," Amber added, then walked toward the kitchen, done with the situation.

Her dismissal seemed to ease the tension in the room. I took my mom's hand and gave it a squeeze. "I think it's safe for me and Max to have some time alone now." I looked to Ida. "Are you okay?"

She gnawed her lower lip, looking worried, but nodded.

My mom gave my hand a final squeeze, then pulled away and went after Amber, shooing my sisters into the kitchen along with her. Ida floated after them.

Max leaned in near my shoulder. "Who were you just talking to?"

I pursed my lips. I'd forgotten that he couldn't see Ida. "My aunt's ghost," I explained.

"You can see ghosts?"

I grinned as I knelt down and picked up Spooky. "Let's sit down. We have a lot to catch up on."

I led the way toward the couch. I still had a lot to deal with—namely two murders, a necromancer, and dark magic—but suddenly I felt like a huge weight had been lifted. Max knew I was a witch, and he was okay with it. I could finally be myself without worrying that he would run the other way.

Of course, now that he was part of my world, he would soon learn about the dangers. Mundanes didn't fare well around magic. There was more than one reason we kept our world a secret.

CHAPTER TWENTY-TWO

I leaned against Max, enjoying the feel of his arm around my shoulders. It had been such a relief to share everything with him. Well—almost everything. I didn't tell him anything about the work I did with Logan. That simply wasn't my secret to tell.

Max glanced at the forgotten bags of ingredients near the door. "You know, you could have just asked me to come over if you didn't actually need to bake."

I laughed. "I panicked. I'm a terrible liar."

"Tell me about it."

I bent my knees up on the couch to turn toward him, more than happy to tell him about it. "Well the other night at dinner, when everyone was acting so strange, it's because my aunt's ghost was messing with things. I didn't have a migraine at all. It was just the first excuse I could think of to get you out of the house."

He chuckled and shook his head. "I've sensed a lot of strange things in my life, but it's still hard to wrap my head around ghosts. Are there any others around besides your aunt?"

I bit my tongue. I hadn't told him about Bradley. That would lead to questions about Logan and the investigation I had promised to keep a secret. An investigation I had already shared too much of with my family out of necessity. "They show up from time to time."

"And what about other witches? Is it just your family?"

Another loaded question. I decided on the safest answer I could think of. "I've met others, but it's rare. Most people who say they're witches might be a little sensitive like you, but they're not like me and my family." I took a sharp breath, realizing something.

Max wrinkled his brow at my expression. "What is it?"

"I just thought of something," I explained. "I need to find my cat."

I hopped up from the sofa. Spooky had eventually left to give us some added privacy. I wasn't sure if me hearing him speak was just a fluke, but now that I had heard some things so clearly, I had to try again.

I found Spooky in the kitchen, sitting on the countertop licking his paw. I didn't see the rest of my family, and hadn't heard them for a while, so they must've gone outside.

I put my elbows on the counter, then leaned down in front of Spooky as Max came into the kitchen behind me.

I concentrated as hard as I could, trying to open my mental pathways. "I need to ask you a question, and I hope you'll answer me," I began. "The other day in the bookstore, after I spoke to Meagan, you said the word *witch*. What did you mean?"

I was met with utter silence. I could feel Max watching us, but he didn't interrupt.

Please, please, please. I thought. *Just tell me what you meant.*

The girl was a witch, Spooky's words echoed through my mind.

My eyes widened. "That's not possible."

A stronger witch than you. She hides it well.

My mouth went dry. If Meagan was a witch, why would she hide it? Unless there were other things she was hiding . . .

She might be strong enough to have killed the warlock, but who can say?

I leaned closer to my cat, peering into his yellow

eyes. "How are you able to speak with me so easily now?"

When you accept your gifts, they work how they're supposed to. Spooky stood up, hopped off the counter, then trotted away.

It seemed he was done speaking with me.

I turned around to find Max still watching me.

"Did you just have an entire conversation with your cat?"

I gave him a nervous smile. "Too weird?"

"A little," he laughed. "Did you learn something important?"

"I'm afraid I did," I admitted. "And I need to make a phone call, in private." As much as I wanted to keep Logan out of my side of things, if Meagan was a danger, he needed to know.

Max crossed his arms. "You're calling the detective, aren't you?"

"Uh . . . " I hesitated.

"He lied for you on several occasions. I'm assuming he knows about things."

I winced. "Yeah, he knows. I would like to tell you more, but there are just some things I'm not supposed to tell anyone."

He watched me for a moment. "Okay, I understand."

I crossed my arms, mirroring him. "You're taking this better than I thought. Most guys wouldn't like it if the woman they're seeing had secrets with another man."

"I can sense emotions, remember?" He grinned.

I stared at him.

"Too weird?" he asked.

"Yeah," I laughed.

He stepped toward me, lowering his arms. "I should get going. I'll let you make your phone call in peace. Call me later?"

I leaned my neck upward as he stepped even closer. "You bet."

He kissed me, and I took a moment to simply enjoy it. Kisses were much nicer when neither party was hiding what they truly were.

CHAPTER TWENTY-THREE

My family came in from the backyard while I waited for Logan to return my call. I'd told them what I had learned about Meagan, and they'd explained that Ida had gone to find Bradley since he had never shown up. I had a bad feeling about both things.

Everyone had gathered at the table while I was making an early dinner when Logan called.

I set my spatula aside, then answered the phone. "Before you say anything, I'm not calling for information. We agreed it was better to keep things separate." It was a stretch, he hadn't really agreed, but I forged on, "Meagan is a witch, one strong enough to hide her magic from me."

He was silent for a moment. "I went by Meagan's shop. She closed early, and the sign says she'll be closed tomorrow too. She's not at her house and her car is gone."

"She said she would be with Jodi and Nina tonight," I explained, "but Logan, if you find her, you shouldn't question her alone. She could be dangerous."

Another long moment of silence. "I know you don't want me to ask, but did you learn anything else from Damon?"

"I don't think he killed his brother, but that's all I know. Bradley was supposed to come back to my house, but he never showed up. We sent Ida to look for him."

More silence.

"Logan—" I hesitated. "I have a feeling there's something else you want to tell me."

"I shouldn't tell you."

"Logan," I pressed. "Why are you looking so hard for Meagan?"

He sighed. "There's been another murder. Jodi is dead."

My stomach fell to my feet. I felt eyes on me and turned to find everyone at the table watching me. The smell of burning fish hit my nostrils and I quickly turned off the burner and moved my pan.

"Addy?" he questioned.

I shook my head, though he couldn't see it. "Was it just like Alison?"

"No, this time was different. The only pattern is that she and Alison were friends. Nina is safe. She's under protection."

I had still never discovered what the runes meant, what possible purpose Alison's death could have served. "And Bradley was different too. Still no sign of his body?"

He went quiet again, then asked, "Is your family with you?"

Everyone was staring at me, listening to my half of the conversation. "Yes."

He sighed. "No sign of Bradley. You may as well tell me what else you're working on from your end."

I gnawed my lower lip. If I told him I was going to the party, he'd want to come, but if whatever had killed Bradley was there, I couldn't let that happen. "I don't know yet," I decided. "We'll figure it out once we find Bradley. Do you know the time," I glanced at my family, "that the last crime happened?"

"Her mother found her an hour ago."

My gut twisted. Her poor mother. I had to find out who was doing this. "Let me find Bradley. Maybe he learned something and that's why he hasn't shown up yet."

"You're worried the necromancer got to him."

"Yeah, I'm worried the necromancer is behind all

of this, I just don't know why. I don't know what he's planning."

I heard someone calling Logan's name in the distance through the phone. His next question was barely above a whisper, "Do you think his plan will come to fruition tonight?"

Let's see, would the necromancer, someone who could control the dead, use the night where the dead were most active and available to enact his evil plot? "I think so."

"You shouldn't be alone tonight, at all."

I looked to my family again. "I won't be. Everyone is here. With a full coven, I should be safe."

"So you'll stay home all night?"

I hesitated, once again debating telling him about the party. "Sure."

"Good, I have to go. Call me when you find Bradley."

He hung up before I could say anything else.

"What happened?" my mom asked. "What other crime?"

I shook my head. "Tonight we're going to find that necromancer, and end him."

Both of my sisters looked at me with wide eyes.

"Even when the victim is a necromancer," Callie began, "it's still murder."

I set my phone on the counter, glancing at the pan

of fried fish I had prepared. Suddenly I had lost my appetite. "We let the police arrest him before, and he easily escaped. We can't let him escape again."

Amber stood from her seat at the table. "He won't be escaping, Adelaide. Don't you worry." She exchanged a meaningful look with my mom.

Luna looked back and forth between the two of them. "What aren't you telling us?"

My mom wasn't meeting any of our eyes.

Amber moved to her side and patted her shoulder, then looked to each of us. "All you girls need to know, is that this isn't our first rodeo."

I stood staring at my mom, jaw agape, dinner entirely forgotten. If I didn't know any better, I'd think Amber was trying to tell us that she and my mom had killed someone before.

When my mom didn't say anything, I knew it was the truth.

Ida appeared near the back door, taking in our stunned silence. "I'd ask what's wrong, but there's no time. Bradley and Damon are both missing."

I stared at her. "What do you mean, *missing*?"

Ida put her hands on her hips. "I mean missing, as in Damon and his car are gone, and I can't sense Bradley anywhere."

Callie glanced around at each of us. "What do we do now?"

Luna stood and walked past me toward the pan of forgotten fish. "We eat, and we get ready for the party. Whatever is going on, we end this tonight."

Callie looked like she might be sick. "And if we find the murderer?"

Luna opened the cabinet to take out plates for everyone. "We deal with it."

My mom was watching me steadily. *Are you okay?* she mouthed.

I nodded, my movements too quick to be convincing. If whatever killed Bradley had gotten to Damon, we were dealing with someone or something extremely powerful. Suddenly having a full coven didn't seem like enough. Not even close.

Luna bumped me with her hip, then handed me a full plate. "Eat up. We need all of our strength for tonight. Callie and I will pick up our familiars before we head to the party."

I carried my plate to the table and sat next to my mom while Amber and my sisters started questioning Ida. I wasn't sure if I could eat.

I looked over to my mom. "Mom, I'm—"

She placed her hand on top of mine. "I know," she muttered. "Me too."

I shivered. Me being scared was one thing, but my mom? She had been in the room when Damon displayed his powers. She knew how strong he was. If he was dead, what chance did the rest of us stand?

I HAD FORCED my dinner down, then excused myself to get ready for the party. I still wasn't thrilled with the costume, but at least it gave me something else to focus on. Spooky stayed in my room with me while I got dressed.

Once I had squeezed into the catsuit, I moved toward my full length mirror to put on the wig and mask. I'd already done my make-up, heavy on the eyes to make them blend in with the mask, and had put my hair in multiple braids to twirl around my head. It was the only thing I could think of to fit them underneath the wig.

I flipped the black hair upside down, then slipped it over my head. Once everything was in place and I looked back into the mirror, I barely recognized myself. The black hair made me look even paler than usual, and would've looked out of place without the black eye make up. I put the delicate mask over my face, securing the thin black ribbons behind my head.

I did a little twirl in front of the mirror. I had to admit, Callie had done a good job. No one would recognize me.

I put a few necessities into a little black clutch, then left my room with Spooky following close behind.

The sun was setting beyond the windows as I descended the stairs into my living room, finding the rest of my family waiting for me. I widened my eyes and covered my mouth, trying not to laugh as I observed the other costumes.

Amber held a finger encased in a furry glove out toward me. "One word about the costumes and I'll hex you."

I believed her, so I kept my hand over my mouth, muffling my laughter. Amber's was the worst since she had a big fluffy lion's mane covering her hair instead of a wig. Of course, she had also escaped wearing a catsuit, so I supposed we were even. Her furred body-suit was looser, and instead of a delicate mask, her face was painted.

I gave her one last look up and down, then took in the others. Callie and Luna were cats like me, but Callie was a ginger tabby and Luna was fluffy and gray. I couldn't see my mom's face at all beneath her hooded jumper made to look like a horse.

I smirked at Callie. "You weren't very nice to mom."

She straightened a mask that was the twin of mine, but gold, laced over a straight ginger wig. "Hey, I offered her my costume. She chose the horse."

"I'm not about to fight a necromancer in a catsuit," my mom's muffled voice replied.

I felt it best not to point out that she would look just as ridiculous doing it in a horse suit. I looked to Luna last. Her long silver wig actually suited her, matching her silver mask. Just like me she had done dark makeup around her eyes. None of us would be easily recognizable.

A squawk drew my attention to her familiar, a raven named Ollie, perched on the back of my white sofa.

"He better not poop," I muttered as Calle withdrew her gecko, Sir Vincent, from her furred fanny pack.

While neither of my sisters could communicate with their familiars like I sometimes could with Spooky, the animals still helped increase their powers, and we needed all of the help we could get. Amber, like my mom, didn't have a familiar. Some witches were drawn to animals, some weren't, though my mom and Amber were plenty powerful without them.

Finally, I looked down to Spooky as he twined around my ankles. "Are you ready?"

As long as I don't have to wear a costume.

I grinned, excited to have heard him again. It seemed the channels of communication in my mind were finally open. I wondered if being accepting of myself enough to finally tell the truth to Max was what had done it.

"We should get going," Amber said. "It will be full dark soon, and we want to catch the necromancer before he does whatever he's planning."

"But what if he's not at the party?" Callie asked.

My mom pushed back the hood of her costume to reveal her face. "We'll check there first, then we'll move on."

I nodded along. "And we need to keep an eye out for Meagan. I don't know how she's involved in all of this, but she hid her magic from us for a reason." *And Jodi is dead*, I added silently. Two members of Meagan's coven murdered in the same way. Was that why she was hiding her magic? Was she afraid she would be next?

If we found her tonight, I'd confront her, but the necromancer had to remain my priority. And the dark magic. It had been disturbingly quiet. It brought whole new meaning to the term *the calm before the storm*.

CHAPTER TWENTY-FOUR

I
t took forty-five minutes to reach the party location in Wickenburg. We would have been more comfortable taking two vehicles, but my mom wanted us all to stay together, and none of us were about to argue with her. She and I got out on the driver's side, both of us looking up at the house where the party was already taking place.

It was huge, almost as large as Damon's, with loud music that seemed to pound in rhythm to my heartbeat.

Ida appeared at my other side. "Do you feel that?"

I nodded.

"Magic," Amber said as she came around the car to meet us. "There is magic happening here."

Callie and Luna followed her, then gathered

around us. We all had our masks on or hoods up. No one would recognize us.

"Does everyone have their phones?" my mom asked.

I patted my clutch where I'd stored my car keys. I had my phone on vibrate so I'd be sure to feel it if the music was too loud to hear it ringing. We would split up in the house since we might be too conspicuous together. Well, everyone except me and Callie. Since neither of us had great defensive magic, we would stay together to watch each other's backs. Everyone knew what the necromancer looked like, but Callie and Luna hadn't met Meagan. I'd done my best to describe her, though if she was at the party she would have a lot of explaining to do.

I turned back to the open car door and gestured for Spooky to hop out. He would be a lot less conspicuous than the raven perched on Luna's shoulder.

"Let's go," I breathed. "If none of us find anything, we meet back here in thirty minutes and I'll convince Logan to give me Meagan's address."

I led the way up the driveway as another car of partygoers pulled up behind us. The feeling of magic intensified as we reached the house, and was nearly suffocating as we stepped inside.

Typical Halloween decorations were strewn all around. Fake cobwebs, dangling skeletons, and plastic bats. We walked through a large entry-room and into an absolutely massive living and dining area lined on one side with floor-length windows and a sliding glass door, which led to the backyard. The door was open, letting partygoers in and out as they pleased. Orange and purple lights glowed in the yard, just as heavily decorated as the living room.

My mom, Amber, and Luna dispersed, leaving Callie and I alone. The room was so crowded no one seemed to notice us as we pushed our way toward the open kitchen.

We were almost there when Callie clutched my arm. "Do you see that?" she gasped.

I'd noticed them at the same time she did. Trays of pastries and other sweets just like the ones we had delivered to the Toasty Bean. Goosebumps erupted on my arms at the sight of them.

Callie pushed close as a girl in a devil costume brushed past us. "Why would your friendly spirits supply pastries to a party in Wickenburg?"

I swallowed the lump in my throat. "Unless they didn't come from friendly spirits."

"But we tried everything. It all seemed fine."

I took one long last look at the pastries, then shook my head. "Nothing we can do about that now. Let's search for the necromancer."

I spotted Spooky darting across the floor as we

wove our way through the living room then through the sliding glass door. If he noticed anything, he would find me, and I trusted him to not get caught. The magical pressure lessened once we were outside, and I finally felt able to breathe.

The yard was huge, big enough that I couldn't see the end of it. There were more tables out here with food and alcohol. People in costume congregated all around them. I knew Wickenburg had a much higher population than Twilight Hollow, but I was still a little shocked to see so many people.

"Let's see how far the yard goes," I decided.

Callie nodded too quickly.

"It's going to be okay," I assured. "We're all here. Nothing is going to mess with a full coven."

If only I believed my own words. I started walking so Callie wouldn't see my worry. The further we walked, the less magic I felt. My shoulders had just started to relax when Callie stopped walking.

I turned back to her. "What's wrong?"

She glanced around. "I don't know, I feel strange."

I noticed some of the partygoers around us looking confused as well. At least those with their faces showing. Everyone was in full costume, so with some of them it was hard to tell.

"I don't like this," Callie muttered, her voice trembling.

But whatever she was feeling, I couldn't sense it.

Callie opened her mouth to say more, then she started shrinking. All I could do was watch as her body shrunk down, and suddenly she was an actual cat. She looked up at me and meowed, then the screaming started.

All around us partygoers transformed, some shrinking and some growing, but all of them changing into whatever they were dressed up as. The screams came from the few who didn't change. Some fainted, while others quickly turned tail and ran.

My mind could barely keep up with what was happening. Acting purely on instinct, I picked up the cat that was Callie, then noticed the little furred fanny pack left behind from beneath her. I grabbed it, praying that her familiar was okay within, then staggered away from the chaos. The girl that had been in the devil costume jumped in front of us, pitchfork in hand. Her skin was red and shiny, her teeth sharp.

Clutching the cat with one hand and holding the fanny pack in the other, I stammered over the first spell I could think of, an illusion spell that would make her not see me and Callie.

It worked, she glanced around, then ran off to terrorize someone else. I looped the fanny pack over my shoulder and ran too, tearing off my wig and mask as I carried Callie further into the yard. I kept running, thinking, *Spooky? Spooky where are you?*

Once I was far enough away from the chaos, I darted behind a tree, clutching Callie to my chest as my heart thundered in my ears. I removed one hand from her fur and pulled my little purse around to get my phone. I quickly hit my mom's number. When she didn't answer, I tried Amber, then Luna, but none of them answered. Had they been transformed just like Callie?

Panting and on the verge of panic, I looked up at the full moon, then had to stifle my scream as something brushed across my leg.

It's me, Spooky said into my mind.

I crouched down beside him, showing him Callie. "Is Callie still in here?" I whispered. "Can you hear what she's thinking?" I tensed at the sound of more screams in the distance.

She's in there, but I cannot read her thoughts. She's too afraid.

"What do we do?" I rasped.

Spooky blinked yellow eyes at me. *Find the source of the enchantment.*

I wracked my brain for an answer, but it had all happened so suddenly. Magic of this caliber would take more than just a spell. The caster would need a lock of hair, something from the victim, or the victim would need to . . . my mouth went dry.

"The pastries. The enchantment was in the pastries. But I ate them too, so why didn't I change?"

Perhaps the spell is centered around you. Perhaps the caster did not want you to change.

"There you are," a voice said behind me. "I've been looking for you everywhere."

I recognized the voice, and was sure my face held all of the terror I felt as I turned around. Standing not ten paces away was the necromancer.

I staggered back on instinct, clutching Callie to my chest. Once I realized what I'd done, I regained those lost steps, letting my anger take over. "What did you do?" I hissed. "What did you do to these people?"

His black hair fell across one eye as he gave me a devilish grin. "You mean the spell? You flatter me, but I'm not that powerful."

"You can't honestly expect me to believe you had nothing to do with this." I glanced down at the ginger cat in my arms.

"Oh I had everything to do with it." He splayed one hand back toward the party. "But the spell was a creation of the spirit that hunts you."

I shivered. The screams were dying down. Those left human had either fled, or were hiding. Those had to be the only two options. I couldn't bear the thought of what else might be happening. "You would think after being possessed you would want to run far away from the dark magic."

His grin split his gaunt face in two. "And miss out on such power? I do what I must to achieve my own ends."

Spooky rubbed against my leg. *He is filled with stolen magic. Do not go near.*

I took a step back. If the dark magic was empowering the necromancer . . . "Tell me how to undo the spell," I demanded.

"Do as Atticus bids, and he will free them." He started reaching a long-boned hand inside his black coat.

I removed one arm from Callie to point a finger at him. "Move another inch and I'll hex you here and now. It was the pastries, wasn't it? They were spelled to make everyone who ate them change tonight. But why not me? I ate them too."

"The spell was created around you," he explained. "You were never intended to change."

I shook my head. I needed to buy time, but for what? I couldn't possibly go with him, but if I didn't, what would happen to everyone else who had eaten the pastries? "I don't understand. The dark magic—Atticus—is powerful, but not this powerful."

He tsked at me. "Halloween, and a channeling

witch is near. Weren't you surprised to not be bombarded by spirits?"

My mouth went dry. If he was implying what I thought he was implying— "What did you do?" I growled.

He lifted his nose proudly. "I captured all of the spirits seeking you out and fed them to Atticus. You're not the only witch in town. He enlisted another to entrap you."

"Damon?" I asked.

He snorted. "The warlock? Hardly."

There was only one other witch I could think of. "Meagan."

He inclined his head. "Atticus can grant great power where he chooses. Now no more stalling. Either come with me, or those transformed will remain that way forever."

Do not, Spooky chimed into my mind.

"Yeah," I agreed out loud, taking another step back, "I think I'll just figure out how to break the spell on my own."

The necromancer's smile made me feel sick. "He said you'd say that. Fortunately, he gave me the power to take you against your will." He lifted his hands and suddenly they were glowing with green magic.

I had a feeling I was better off amongst the mundanes transformed into their costumes. I continued backing away. I wanted to run, but I was worried as soon as I turned my back he would throw that magic at me and I would be incapacitated. I couldn't risk it. I needed a distraction.

At first I thought the low growl coming from behind a nearby shrub was my imagination, then a lioness prowled around the foliage. My heart skipped a beat.

The lioness growled again.

"Amber?" I squeaked.

But her attention was on the necromancer.

She says to run, Spooky chimed into my mind. *Your mother and Luna are trying to protect the mundanes at the party. We must reverse the enchantment.*

The necromancer lifted his glowing hands, seeming unsure what to do with the lion. "Don't you dare run away," he said to me.

I hesitated. Amber was giving me the distraction I needed, but what if he hurt her?

She says she'll be fine, Spooky urged.

Thank goddess for chatty cats, I thought, then I turned tail and ran.

CHAPTER TWENTY-FIVE

I ran a wide loop around the party. By the time I reached my car and got both Callie and Spooky inside, I had organized my thoughts.

The dark magic, which now had a name, had recruited Meagan and the necromancer to enchant the pastries. It—he—wanted to use the spell as leverage to make me do his bidding. Since that most certainly wasn't going to happen, I needed to find a way to break the spell on my own. I needed to find Meagan.

I started the car and pulled out onto the street, keeping my eyes open for any enchanted mundanes. While I drove I unzipped the furred fanny pack in my lap. Callie's gecko poked his little head out, unharmed. Even with him near to bolster her magic, Callie had stood no chance against the enchantment.

Where are we going? Spooky asked. He and Callie both sat in the front passenger seat together.

"We need to find Meagan, and I only know one person who can help us do that."

Who?

"A scrying warlock," I answered. "Are you able to communicate with Callie?"

All animals can communicate. It's the humans who struggle.

"Wise ass," I muttered as I took the next turn. "We are going to Damon's house to see if we can figure out where he and Bradley went. I'll need both of you to be on the lookout. I don't want to get caught for breaking and entering." I thought of Ida, and realized she wouldn't have been transformed like the others.

As if on cue, her voice came from the back seat. "Geez Addy, you didn't have to leave without me."

I tightened my grip on the steering wheel. "Is Amber okay? I hated leaving her."

"Amber and the others are fine, but you won't find evidence of Damon at his home. We can't waste the time it would take to look."

I slowed the car, now unsure which direction I should drive in. "So what do we do?"

"We call Logan and get Meagan's address."

My throat felt tight. "We can't involve him."

"He'll be involved regardless when the transformed mundanes start ransacking the city. Call him and tell him what's happening, *now*."

Well, she had a point. I slowed the car and pulled over, making sure to hit the automatic locks in case anyone snuck up on us, then retrieved my cell phone from my purse and called Logan.

"We'll have to make this quick," he answered without saying hello. "We're getting all sorts of crazy calls at the station."

I took a deep breath. "The dark magic, which now has a name, spelled a bunch of pastries to make mundanes transform into their costumes. The necromancer found me and told me I had to come with him, and the dark magic would undo the spell. I . . . um, I ran away."

He was silent for several long seconds.

"Logan?" I questioned.

"Where are you? Are you safe?"

I glanced at the two cats in my passenger seat. "I'm safe, for now, but maybe I should have gone with him."

"And just trust that the spell would get reversed? This thing probably wants to use you for something far worse. You were right to run away."

I hated that I wanted his approval to feel better about my decision, but there it was. Maybe I had made the right choice. "Logan, I need Meagan's address. She helped create the enchantment. I'm going to make her tell me how to reverse it."

He gave it to me without argument, which was perhaps the most shocking thing to happen so far. "I'll meet you there," he added.

"You can't. It's too dangerous. And if I end up having to do something bad to Meagan, you can't know about it."

"I'm not going to let you get yourself killed," he said, then hung up.

"Crap," I muttered, pulling my phone away from my ear. I repeated the address he told me over and over again in my head until I was able to type it into my phone, then hit the GPS. If he insisted on meeting me there, I would just have to get there first and take Meagan somewhere else.

If I could take Meagan somewhere else. Two of her friends were dead, and it was beginning to seem like a real possibility that she was the one who killed them.

AS LUCK WOULD HAVE IT, Meagan's house was only ten minutes away. I shut off the headlights as I drove up the pitch dark driveway, sandwiched by tall trees. The property bordered dense forest. Even though I hadn't spotted the house yet, I ventured a guess that Meagan was even more wealthy than

Damon, which didn't quite make sense given her occupation.

The thought that maybe this was a family home made me hit the brakes. If Meagan was a witch, she might have a mother and sisters. She might even have a full coven waiting for me. Maybe I should have taken my chances with the dark magic and necromancer after all.

We should park here, Spooky said into my mind. *Remain unseen. I can scout ahead for you.*

"I'm really glad I can finally hear you," I said to him, then turned around in my seat to look at Ida. I voiced my fears about Meagan's family.

"Leave it to me," she said. "I'll go into the house and check around."

She disappeared, and I turned back to the two cats. "I need you two to find me a discreet path up to the house."

What do you intend to do when we find her? Spooky asked.

I felt like I was channeling Luna as an air of grim determination overtook me. "I'm going to make her reverse the enchantment, whatever it takes. No one turns my family into animals and gets away with it."

I moved the car as far off the driveway as I could, then put it in park and shut off the engine. I checked on Sir Vincent in his fanny pack one more time, then

CHAPTER TWENTY-SIX

The path through the woods led to a small cabin, appearing even more abandoned than the house. The windows were all broken and the front door hung slightly ajar. Only it wasn't abandoned, I could feel what Ida had sensed.

Death magic. *Necromancy.*

Had I escaped the necromancer only to walk right into his trap?

Spooky pressed against my leg. *I believe they are underground. Perhaps a cellar.*

I was too scared to speak out loud. *Find it*, I thought.

I jumped at a buzzing sound, then realized my phone had gone off in my pocket.

I checked it to find a text from Logan, asking where I was.

While I had originally hoped to exclude Logan, suddenly the idea of a detective with a gun sounded highly appealing. I wanted to protect him, but at what cost? If I found Meagan and she killed me, there would be no one left to make her break the enchantment.

A cabin behind the house, I typed back. *We're looking for a cellar.*

Don't go in without me.

Just as I read Logan's text, Spooky hopped out of a broken window. *There is a trap door inside.*

I lifted my phone. *Trap door in the cabin,* I typed, then put it back in my pocket.

"Let's go," I whispered to Ida and the cats.

I approached the cabin and placed my hands on the door, but couldn't sense any wards. Despite the door hanging crookedly, it opened easily and I stepped inside. Fresh footprints marred the coating of dust on the wood floor.

With only a few pieces of broken furniture in the cabin and moonlight streaming through the windows, it was easy to spot the trap door. Although, it was large enough I knew I might have trouble lifting it.

Ida floated near my shoulder, her eyes on the trap door. "I'll go down first," she whispered.

My throat tight, I nodded. "Be careful," I whispered back, and then she was gone.

I waited what seemed like an eternity, but was met

with only silence. Ida didn't return. Logan would reach the cabin soon and I wanted to at least go in ahead of him. I could take the brunt of any magical attacks and hopefully he could rescue me if I needed it.

When roughly five minutes had passed and Ida still hadn't returned, I tiptoed to the trap door. I knelt beside it, then placed my ear to the ground. I could just barely hear muffled voices. Either the floor was more insulated than one might guess, or whatever space lay below was large enough for the voices to be far away.

Betting my life on the latter, I gripped the handle of the trap door with both hands and tugged. My back strained against the heavy wood and I nearly pulled a muscle as I shuffled my feet along the floor, moving to the other side of the door to lay it gently on the ground.

I could hear the voices more clearly now, but they were definitely further away. Perhaps within a separate room below.

I peered down a dark stairway, barely lit by a battery-powered lantern.

Callie and I will go first, Spooky said into my mind.

I shook my head, then thought, *No, something happened to Ida down there. I'm not going to lose either of you. We go together.*

I took the first few steps, my palms sweating as I gripped the handrail further down. The room below was small and bare, ending in a single door. The voices grew louder as I reached it.

I recognized Meagan first. "I won't help you anymore. This has gone too far."

"It's too late to back out now. Our guest of honor is almost here."

I froze with my hand halfway to the door knob. The second voice was the necromancer, and he knew I was here. He had never intended to take me from the party at all. He knew once he told me Meagan was involved in the enchantment, I would come looking for her.

His voice sounded right on the other side of the door. "You may as well come inside, Adelaide."

Hide, I thought to Spooky, then I opened the door and stepped inside.

Megan stood near the necromancer, still wearing the sleek black dress I had seen her in earlier. Only now her hair was a mess and her eyes were puffy. "I'm sorry," she blurted.

The necromancer cut her off with a raised hand, then gestured to the other side of the room. "You're just in time to play your part." The door slammed shut of its own volition behind me.

I jumped at the sound of the door, then my eyes reflexively followed his outstretched hand. My blood went cold. Damon was chained to the wall, a thick swath of black fabric gagging him. His head hung limp to one side. He still wore his button up shirt and slacks, both now stained with grime.

Beside him was a pulsing green light, like the dark magic, but . . . brighter. Even more powerful.

My gut clenched, because I could sense what was inside it. All of the spirits that should've been visiting me over Halloween were trapped in the magical mass. The necromancer had trapped them, and I had a feeling Ida was in there now too. Even as a living mortal, the magic tugged at me. The green light floated closer to Damon, but he still didn't move.

"He's not dead," the necromancer said before I could ask. "After dear Megan killed the first one, I had to put her on a tighter leash."

I turned wide eyes to Meagan. "You killed Bradley? You were strong enough to covertly take down a warlock in broad daylight?

Tears fell down her cheeks. "I thought he killed Alison." She whipped a finger toward the necromancer. "*He* told me Bradley killed her. He said runes from the Celtic Ogham were painted with her blood. The Maxwell's follow the Celtic tradition."

"Dear Meagan has air magic," he explained. "I only wanted her to trap the other warlock so we could use him. But she was so upset she crushed him until his insides oozed out."

I put a hand to my chest, picturing the bloody hiking boot. "If Bradley was useless to you dead, why bother hiding the body?"

Meagan was crying so hard her words were unintelligible.

The necromancer smirked. "Meagan panicked and sent him down a river. I fetched him so I could lure his brother here tonight."

I felt like I was going to be sick. "You left Bradley's boot in Damon's yard for him to find. It had traces of Meagan's magic for him to track."

"Yes," the necromancer drawled. "Of course, you foiled that plan. Fortunately, the warlock was more clever than I gave him credit for. He didn't need my help to find us."

I shook my head as the pieces slowly fell into place. "You killed Alison just to manipulate Meagan, then she killed Bradley, thinking she was avenging her friend. But who killed Jodi?"

Meagan gasped through her tears, "Jodi is dead?"

The necromancer laughed. "As I said, the warlock was more clever than I gave him credit for. Damon figured out that Meagan was interfering with his scrying. He tracked her magic to her friend's house."

The room felt like it was spinning. Damon was a jerk, but I really didn't think he would kill anyone. Of course, he thought he was killing his brother's murderer.

"What is all of this for?" I rasped. "Why did you want the warlocks to begin with?"

The necromancer stepped toward me. "You've deduced so much, and *that's* what's stumping you?"

I glanced at Damon, then the green magic, then back to the necromancer. "Yeah, that really is what's stumping me."

"Atticus is the spirit of an ancient warlock," he explained. "He needs a suitable vessel. He tried to take me, but my magic comes from the spirits. He needed someone whose magic came from within."

I stopped breathing. He needed Bradley or Damon. He was trying to come back into this world in a mortal vessel.

The necromancer watched my expression. "I see you understand. Atticus cast Damon from your home because he was worried you might harm each other, and you are both needed for what is to come."

I stepped a little further from Damon and the green magic, shaking my head over and over. I couldn't tear my eyes away from the mass of spirits as I spoke. "You used all of the spirits to empower Atticus, and now you want me to put that whole thing inside of Damon to take him over."

I jumped as the necromancer was suddenly right

by my side. "Between the two of us, we should be able to manage. Do as I say, and the enchantment will be ended. Do anything else, and everyone transformed tonight will remain that way forever."

I struggled to take a full breath. "But you can't do that. You can't expose all this magic to the world. If you leave them like they are, there will be no way to contain it."

"Atticus has no intention of hiding once he has returned. We do not care what the mundanes see, nor how they are affected." He placed one bony hand on my shoulder. "Now make your choice, witch, the night wears on."

My shoulders shook as I fought back tears. My family, everyone at the party, anyone who had eaten pastries . . . I couldn't leave them that way. But could I sacrifice Damon to save them? Could I let Atticus return?

I took a deep breath, managing to contain my emotions. "Let's get this over with."

CHAPTER TWENTY-SEVEN

The necromancer grabbed my arm, dragging me toward the green magic. I was glad Damon was unconscious. He didn't need to see what was coming for him.

The necromancer extended his free hand back toward Meagan. "Come," he ordered.

She wiped her red-rimmed eyes and shook her head. "No, I told you I won't help you anymore."

The necromancer let go of my arm and stormed toward her, his hand lifted like he might strike her.

"What's in all of this for you?" I blurted, trying to distract him. "Who even are you?"

He lowered his hand and glanced over his shoulder at me. "Power, of course. My own power. No more stealing. Atticus can grant me all of my desires." He hesitated. "As for who I am, that's of no relevance."

He turned back to Meagan. "You will finish what you started, or you will die."

A tickling sensation up my spine made me realize how close I had gotten to the big ball of magic. I could sense Atticus, but I could also sense the ghosts.

Help me, Addy, Ida's voice breezed through my mind. *If you fight for control of the spirits, they will go to you. They will choose you over him.*

I fought to keep a straight face as the necromancer lost his patience and dragged Meagan across the room.

"I won't help you!" she screamed, dragging her feet across the aged wood floor.

Logan is here, Spooky mentally warned me.

Stall him, I thought back.

"What are you looking at?" the necromancer demanded.

I realized I had been involuntarily staring at the door.

"Would you truly run and leave your family as animals?" he pressed.

I steeled my expression. "Let's get this over with. Just tell me what to do."

I walked closer to the green magic, feeling the ghosts trying to reach out to me only to be reined in again by Atticus. To my horror, Damon opened his eyes. It took him a moment to focus, then his eyes darted wildly around the room. "Where am I?" he gasped.

He stared at me first, then his attention turned to Meagan. "*You!*" He struggled against the chains holding him in place. "You're the one who killed my brother!"

She tore her arm away from the necromancer. "And you killed Jodi!"

"Silence," the necromancer hissed. He looked to me. "You will need to channel the spirits as a whole, but you will only place Atticus in the warlock's body. Use the other spirits as fuel to grant yourself enough power to do so."

I blinked at him. "I think you've grossly overestimated me. I don't know how to do that."

"You will figure it out, or we will not undo the enchantment."

I looked past him to Meagan. She had stopped crying and watched me with her chin lowered, trying to tell me something with her eyes.

Was she trying to tell me she was capable of removing the enchantment herself?

But even if she could, that still left all of the spirits trapped by Atticus. I couldn't leave them, and I most certainly couldn't use them as fuel. They weren't objects.

You're strong enough, Addy, Ida's voice barely

reached me, like it was coming from somewhere far away.

"I'm strong enough," I muttered, turning to face Damon and the green magic.

"What are you doing?" Damon demanded. "Let me go right this instant, and free Bradley."

So Bradley was in the mass of magic too, that's why he hadn't come to find me.

"You shouldn't have gone after Jodi," I said to Damon. "You should have told me your suspicions before you killed the wrong girl."

He cringed. "I tracked the magic there. I really thought it was her."

I shook my head and turned toward the green magic. "You deserve whatever happens to you." I wasn't sure of the right way to do things. I only really knew one way to channel, *touch*. I took a deep breath, then stepped into the mass of magic.

"What are you doing!" I heard the necromancer cry, but his voice was suddenly far away. It was like stepping into a big green bubble. While it pulsed with magic on the outside, inside it was calm, and impossibly large. Much larger than the room which contained it. Spirits floated around aimlessly.

I stepped further into the space, searching for Ida.

"Atticus won't let her come to you," a male voice said directly beside me.

I turned to look at Bradley, his features barely distinguishable. He was just a shadow of his former self, weakened to power the necromancer's spells.

"Please save my brother. He was only trying to avenge me. I tried to stop him."

I shook my head. "This isn't about Damon, but I'll spare him if I can."

I had been hoping to find Ida, she could at least tell me what to do. In life, her magic had been the same as mine. I closed my eyes and reached out my hands, sensing the surrounding spirits.

"Come to me," I whispered.

I felt a connection to the spirits, but it wasn't right. They were clinging to me, trying to break free of what held them. Atticus was keeping them from me.

I felt a small hole form in the prison, and whirled around, searching for the source.

Spooky trotted toward me. *You must hurry. I could not delay Logan. The necromancer will harm him.*

My heart sputtered. "I don't know what to do. Atticus has trapped all the spirits. He's not going to let me summon them until he believes I'm going to help him."

Spooky pressed against my leg. *You are a channeling witch, Adelaide O'Shea. He is a long-dead warlock. Show him what good witches do to bad warlocks.*

Bradley took my hand, though he didn't have much of a hand himself, it was more like a feeling of cool mist brushing my skin. "I don't have much strength to give, but take all of it. I can move on if it means you'll save my brother."

I didn't have time to question his offer. Spooky was right. I was a channeling witch, and I was alive. I was done being terrified of some long-dead warlock.

I channeled Bradley's ghost, then used the power to reach out to the others. What I was doing was technically necromancy, but I saw no other choice.

It was time to send Atticus to the afterlife.

CHAPTER TWENTY-EIGHT

The feel of spirits rushing into me made me sway on my feet. Atticus' power closed in around me a moment later, trying to invade me with the rest of them. I forced the heavy, sickly feel of his magic away, and it was . . . easy. Still trapped inside his magical bubble, I could feel his confusion. He had wanted me to take in the spirits, but he hadn't expected me to be able to keep him out.

He hadn't been expecting me to create magic from the spirits, just like—my next thought almost made me lose focus. I wasn't just doing something similar to necromancy, this was necromancy. I wasn't just a channelling witch, I was a *necromancer*. A channeling witch could only channel. A necromancer could control spirits, and could convert their energy into power.

Don't worry about it now, Spooky said into my mind, though I could hardly hear him over the roaring power. *Time is short.*

He was right. I could worry about the implications of what I was doing later. I gathered all the magic of the spirits within me, then forced a portion of it outward, hitting the wall of the bubble. It was as easy as exhaling.

With a loud pop, I was back in the cellar, which was now filled with roiling green fog. Spooky stood near my feet.

First I spotted Logan on the floor. He wasn't moving. Still a cat, Callie crouched beside him. Then my attention was drawn to Meagan and Damon—the latter now free from his shackles—both facing the necromancer. Magic swarmed around them all. If a mundane saw the scene, they might feel a bit of an unnatural wind, but that was it. But as a channeling witch, the magic filled my senses, sticking to the back of my tongue like the smell of fresh rain after a drought.

The necromancer lifted his hands, prepared to send a hex toward Meagan and Damon.

I sent a wave of magic at him, just like I had done inside the bubble. It blasted him from his feet, slamming him into the wall. He slid down it, landing with his long legs askew on the floor.

He blinked up at me through the green fog as I approached him. "How? You shouldn't be able to use the spirits' magic in such a way."

I stood over him, highly aware of Atticus' presence still in the room, but with the sheer volume of magic I was holding, the long-dead warlock couldn't touch me. He and the necromancer had unknowingly provided me with the power I needed to defeat them. It was so intoxicating I could understand why the necromancer was obsessed with obtaining more.

"Think about it," I said to him.

He just stared up at me.

Behind us, Damon said, "You're a necromancer, but you're also a witch. You have two types of magic, but that's—"

"Impossible," Meagan finished for him.

For the first time, real fear shone in the necromancer's eyes. "What are you going to do to me?"

I smiled. "Set things right." I wasn't even sure if the words were my own. With so much magic inside of me, I felt like I was channeling a thousand different voices.

With a thought, I sent all the magic outward, releasing the spirits. It was the type of power the necromancer had always hoped for, but could never have because there was one difference. The spirits helped me willingly.

The magic passed through him, freeing those he

still held captive, taking every last ounce of power he had acquired. The magic continued outward, out into Wickenburg and Twilight Hollow.

Meagan gasped the moment her enchantment broke.

I turned to find her leaning heavily against Damon, then they both seemed to realize they were touching each other and staggered away.

The necromancer stared up at me, dazed. The green fog that was Atticus was nowhere to be seen.

"You are evil," Damon hissed.

I glared at him. "You murdered an innocent girl. I don't think you have any room to throw stones."

That shut him up as I knelt by Logan's side, turning him onto his back.

He groaned, lifting his hand to a welt near his temple. It took his dark eyes a moment to focus on me. "What happened?"

I forced a smile, though I felt shaken to my bones. Now that the magic of the spirits had left me, I was faced with the harsh reality of what I had become. What I supposed I always was. "It's over now. And you have all three of your murderers here to arrest if you can stand."

"Now wait just a—" Damon began.

I cut him off with a warning glare. "You did just see what happened to the necromancer, right? Don't make me do it to you." It was an idle threat. I didn't think I could wipe out Damon's magic, but he didn't need to know that.

He took a step back, going quiet.

"Not to interrupt," Callie's voice came from outside the now open the door, "but I could really use some clothing."

Logan blinked at me, waiting for an explanation. Callie must have lost her clothes when she was transformed back to normal.

"Can you sit up?" I said to Logan as I leaned away and removed my coat.

His eyes went even wider at his first glimpse of the catsuit underneath.

"Kindly avert your gaze and arrest the murderers," I said as I stood.

I moved toward the door, aiming a glare at each of them, though the necromancer was just staring into space. "I will expect you all to cooperate," I warned, "or else."

I went to offer my coat to my sister, while Logan finally stood to arrest the murderers.

Everyone cooperated. Imagine that.

CHAPTER TWENTY-NINE

The next morning found me and my family safe in my home, some of us sprawled on the furniture, while Callie laid flat on her back on the floor. Spooky lounged across the arm of the sofa, fast asleep.

Ida had gathered enough power to return around sunrise. Now that Halloween was over, she'd soon have to go back to haunting the woods near my mom's house. Not that she minded. She had declared me an utter handful and was glad to go back to her more relaxed existence, even if it meant no more pranks on mundanes until next year.

"I feel like I have a hangover," Callie groaned, "and I didn't even get to have one drink."

My mom nursed a cup of coffee on the couch

beside me. She still wore her loose flannel pajamas with her ginger waves frothing around her face. "At least you didn't spend your night running around as a horse trying to corral the mundanes. It's a miracle no one got killed."

"It's a miracle Amber didn't do the killing," Luna sniffed from one of the adjacent chairs.

Amber lounged in the other chair like a contented cat. "I quite liked being a lioness. Perhaps that Meagan can teach me the enchantment so I can try it again."

I leaned back with my coffee mug clutched in both hands. "*That Meagan* will be going to prison for murdering Bradley. She won't be around to teach you any spells."

"And Bradley is gone?" Luna asked.

Callie lifted her head off the floor to meet my waiting gaze. Explaining to Damon that his brother had moved on without saying goodbye had not been a comfortable situation. But it was what Bradley had wanted. He had helped me save everyone, and helped me to put his murderer behind bars.

Of course, I felt a little bad for Meagan. She felt awful about killing the wrong man. She had admitted everything to the police, well almost everything. She couldn't exactly explain *how* she had killed Bradley. Her family came back early from a vacation to hire her the best lawyer money could buy.

Damon, on the other hand, was denying everything. He had lawyered up too, and of course, he hardly knew Jodi, and there was no actual evidence against him. He would probably go free, but I would be watching him.

"You look like you're going to go all necromancer scary again," Callie commented.

My expression softened, and I sipped my coffee. "Please don't remind me. I don't even want to think about that."

My mom placed her hand on my knee. "We can't avoid it. This same magic drove that man crazy, and you possess more than he ever did."

Suddenly my comforting coffee had my stomach in knots. The police had identified the necromancer as a man named Malcolm Watts. He had been a normal kid growing up. His mother reported him missing when he was sixteen. He had suddenly started staring at walls and speaking gibberish, and then she never saw him again. He left on his quest to accumulate power and had never looked back.

It could happen to me too. I had felt how addictive the power was. I never wanted to touch that kind of magic again. No, that was a part of me I planned on sealing away forever. Max was coming over soon to hear the whole story, but not the *whole* story. I would be leaving out the necromancer part. He hadn't dressed up for Halloween, so he wouldn't have been changed, but he still had no memories of the previous night. No one in town did except us magical folk, and Logan . . . though quite a few people remembered waking up naked.

We weren't sure why the memories were erased, but it must've had something to do with breaking such a powerful enchantment. Logan had likely only been spared because he was so close to me when I sent the magic out.

A knock on the door had me setting aside my coffee to stand. Out of all of us, I was somehow feeling the best. Of course, I hadn't been transformed into an animal.

I opened the door to find not Max, but Logan waiting outside. He wore his usual suit, and his unmarked police car was parked out on the street. The welt on his head had blossomed into a large purple bruise.

"You know, I could fix a poultice for that," I commented.

He raised his hands. "Please, no more magic. I just wanted to stop by and see for myself that you were all okay." He glanced past me to everyone gathered in the living room. He turned his attention back to me. "And I also wanted to thank you. For saving my life, and for solving my case. It was a real doozy."

I chuckled at his choice of words. "Don't mention it. I'm always glad to help."

"You'll let me know if the dark magic comes back? I want to be prepared for its next scheme."

I nodded. I wasn't sure how much damage I had done to Atticus, but I suspected he had fled, knowing he had lost. But there would always be other opportunities. "And let me know if you need any help with Damon or Meagan."

"Let's hope I don't need any more of your help any time soon. Maybe we could just have a nice, normal dinner sometime instead."

I lifted my brows at the offer, just as Max pulled up on the street and got out of his jeep.

Logan turned to watch him as he approached, then looked back to me. "I'll be in touch, Ms. O'Shea."

I nodded with a small smile. "Detective White."

Logan waved to Max as they passed each other, then I stepped away from the door for Max to come inside.

I thought about how I was going to explain all of the events of the previous night to him, and realized it didn't matter how much or how little I told him. He would believe me.

He could spend the day with me and my family, and he wouldn't go running for the hills . . . and neither would Logan.

I might have just found out that I was a necro-mancer, but at least I had a nice support system.

Like usual, I was going to need all of the help I could get.

ALSO BY SARA C. ROETHLE

TREE OF AGES

Finn doesn't know what—or who—uprooted her from her peaceful tree form, changing her into this clumsy, disconnected human body. All she knows is she is cold and alone until Àed, a kindly old conjurer, takes her in.

By the warmth of Àed's hearth fire, vague memories from her distant past flash across her mind, sparking a restless desire to find out who she is and what powerful magic held her in thrall for over a century.

As Finn takes to the road, she and Àed accumulate a ragtag band of traveling companions. Historians, scholars, thieves in disguise, and Iseult, a mercenary of few words whose silent stare seems to pierce through all of Finn's defenses.

The dangers encountered unleash a wild magic Finn never knew she possessed, but dark forces are

pulled mercilessly into a plot to overthrow the Empire, and to save the elven races from meeting a bloody end.

Elmerah will learn of a dark magical threat, and will have to face the thing she fears most: the duplicitous older sister she left behind, far from their home in Shadowmarsh.

Books in the series:
The Witch of Shadowmarsh
Curse of the Akkeri
The Elven Apostate
Empire of Demons
Legend of the Arthali
Gods of Twilight

THE WILL OF YGGDRASIL

The first time Maddy accidentally killed someone, she passed it off as a freak accident. The second time, a coincidence. But when she's kidnapped and taken to an underground realm where corpses reanimate on their own, she can no longer ignore her dark gift.

The first person she recognizes in this horrifying realm is her old social worker from the foster system, Sophie, but something's not right. She hasn't aged a day. And Sophie's brother, Alaric, has fangs and moves with liquid feline grace.

A normal person would run screaming into the night, but there's something about Alaric that draws Maddy in. Together, they must search for an elusive magical charm, a remnant of the gods themselves. Maddy doesn't know if she can trust Alaric with her life, but with the entire fate of humanity hanging in the balance, she has no choice.

Books in the series:

Fated

Fallen

Fury

Forged

Found

THE THIEF'S APPRENTICE

Liliana is trapped alone in the dark. Her father is dead, and London is very far away. If only she hadn't been locked up in her room, reading a book she wasn't allowed to read, she might have been able to stop her father's killer. Now he's lying dead in the next room, and there's nothing she can do to bring him back.

Arhyen is the self-declared finest thief in London. His mission was simple. Steal a journal from Fairfax Breckinridge, the greatest alchemist of the time. He hadn't expected to find Fairfax himself, with a dagger in his back. Nor had he expected the alchemist's automaton daughter, who claims to have a soul.

Suddenly entrenched in a mystery too great to fully comprehend, Arhyen and Liliana must rely on the help of a wayward detective, and a mysterious masked man, to piece together the clues laid before them. Will they uncover the true source of Liliana's soul in time, or will London plunge into a dark age of nefarious technology, where only the scientific will survive?

Books in the series:
Clockwork Alchemist
Clocks and Daggers
Under Clock and Key

Printed in Great Britain
by Amazon